BAYOU HEAT

ALEXANDRA IVY

LAURA WRIGHT

Editor: Julia Ganis, JuliaEdits.com
Cover Art by Patricia Schmitt (Pickyme)
Formatting by Sweet 'N Spicy Designs

MICHEL

ALEXANDRA IVY

CHAPTER 1

Winter was no more than a crisp edge in the breeze that threaded its way through the Wildlands. Michel sucked in a deep breath of the fresh air, savoring the tingle of magic that flowed through his veins.

He loved this secret homeland of the Pantera. It was a place of beauty, power, and untamed dangers that lurked in the thick shadows. Not even the dozen new houses that were being constructed for the victims who'd been rescued from Locke's dungeons of horror could mar the lush wetlands that were filled with a vibrant green.

This morning, however, his attention wasn't on the cypress trees that dotted the thick bayous, or the nearby cubs who playfully wrestled on a patch of grass. Instead he watched the slender female who was perched on a fallen log, monitoring the playful cubs and occasionally making scratches on a clipboard she had balanced on her knees.

She was a striking beauty with her long curly red hair that blazed in the sunlight with a rich gold threaded through the strands. Her eyes were a pale green and her skin was soft and satiny, except for the scars that ran from her mid-cheek down to her throat.

The first time he'd seen her, he'd noticed the burn marks she tried to hide with her hair, but he'd instantly dismissed them. Instead, it was the rest of her satin skin that had captured and held his attention. A perfect cream that made his cat long to lick it until it was rosy with passion.

His intense arousal had set off all sorts of alarms in the back of his mind. Not to mention pissed him off.

This female had worked with Locke, kidnapping and torturing his people, along with innocent humans. And for all he knew, she was still working for the bastard.

It was obscene that his cat would instantly fall in lust with her.

And even more obscene he'd been unable to take another female to his bed since she'd arrived in the Wildlands nearly a month before.

He swallowed a growl as he sensed the approach of his leader.

Like him, Raphael was a Suit, but the two males couldn't be more different. Raphael was tall, with a golden beauty and easy charm that made him the perfect Diplomat. Michel, on the other hand, was three inches shorter with broad shoulders and muscles that bulged beneath the New Orleans Saints sweatshirt and faded jeans he was wearing. His dark hair was skull-shaved and his eyes a dark green rimmed with black. His skin was naturally a deep copper tone, with a tattoo of a crouching puma inked on his chest.

He was also more aggressive than most Suits, which was why his brothers had been shocked when Raphael had made him a spy. But while Michel might not have a golden tongue, or the ability to mix among the humans, he could scale a building, disable the surveillance, and take out a dozen guards without breaking a sweat. Hell, he'd broken into the Oval Office just to prove he could.

"Should I ask why you spend so much time watching Dr. Young?" Raphael demanded, folding his arms over his chest as he studied Michel's tight expression.

"I would think that was obvious," he muttered.

"Yes, I suppose it is," Raphael drawled. "She's lovely."

A strange sensation tightened around Michel's chest, his gaze never wavering from the female. She wasn't lovely.

She was stunning.

It wasn't just the delicate features or the fiery hair. It was the intense intelligence that shimmered in her green eyes and the grim resolution etched on her face.

This female was a survivor.

His cat was dangerously fascinated. Thankfully, his brain was connected to his human side. Which meant he wasn't going to be blinded by a pretty face and perfect tits.

"I don't trust her," he said, his voice hard as he watched her lean forward and lightly run a finger down the nearest cub's back.

Over the past two weeks she'd requested the opportunity to do non-invasive research on the children who had been created in Locke's laboratories. She'd promised that she only wanted to make sure that they were healthy and growing at a steady rate.

"Have you forgotten that she has given us information on our enemy that we would never have discovered without her?" Raphael demanded. "And that her skills have helped us heal our people?"

Michel turned his head to meet Raphael's determinedly bland expression. Were his lips twitching?

Did the annoying shit think Michel's obsession with the female was funny?

"She's shared just enough to earn a place in the Wildlands," Michel snapped. "For all we know she's a very clever spy who's trying to lull us into complacency while she gathers intel to send to our enemies."

"So cynical," Raphael murmured.

"Because it's what I would do," Michel said between clenched teeth.

"True."

Michel made a sound of frustration. He didn't understand why everyone else was so eager to forgive and forget when it came to Dr. Chelsea Young.

She was the enemy.

No matter what his cat might be trying to tell him.

"Besides, she's had Pantera blood. She's admitted that she's developed heightened senses and she's stronger than she was before her injections," he pressed. "And there's that little matter of her claim that she can 'sense' the Pantera. And even humans from a great distance."

Raphael shrugged, not nearly as concerned as he should be. "I know, which is why I have her under constant surveillance."

He nodded toward a large Hunter with short, tousled dark hair and eyes that were a vivid violet flecked with gold.

Far from comforted, Michel growled deep in his throat.

The young male had been lurking around Chelsea for weeks, his handsome features and easy charm easily working their magic on Dr. Young. Usually Michel found Rage's ability to ensnare the opposite sex a source of amusement.

Now there was nothing funny about it.

Not one fucking thing.

"Rage is a talented Hunter, but he doesn't understand the complex games that spies play,"

Michel pointed out the obvious. "Not too mention he's a perpetual flirt."

Raphael cocked a brow. "Does that bother you?"

Michel refused to be goaded. He'd already revealed more than he wanted. "It leaves him open to manipulation."

"Ah." There was a hesitation before Raphael cleared his throat. "You know, Michel, I assumed you of all people would be sympathetic to Chelsea."

His brows snapped together. "Why would I have sympathy for a woman who used our people as science experiments?"

"Because you know what it's like to be different while you're growing up, and the desperation to fit in."

Michel's breath caught in his throat, his cat crouching inside him as a remembered pain made him flinch. He rarely allowed himself to recall his early childhood when he'd been born with deformed legs. The twisted joints had been beyond the efforts of the Healers, and it hadn't been until human technology had evolved far enough to operate on him that he'd at last been able to walk.

Yes. He understood the dark desperation of being flawed. And the fierce need to do whatever to gain command of your life. And why Chelsea's eyes remained shadowed even when she smiled…

"It's not at all the same," he abruptly denied.

"No?"

His fists clenched. “I didn’t sacrifice others for my cure.”

Raphael gave a dip of his head. “Fair enough.”

Michel turned so he was facing his companion. “When are you going to confess what’s going on, Raphael?”

The older male shrugged. “What makes you think something is going on?”

Michel gave a short laugh. “I can sense when you’re tap-dancing around because you have a piece of shit duty you’re about to dump on me.”

“Okay.” Raphael grinned. “I need you.”

“About damned time,” Michel breathed. As much as he loved the Wildlands, he needed to get away and clear his head.

Plus he needed to be doing *something*. Anything.

“You might not be so eager when I explain your mission,” Raphael warned.

Michel gave a lift of his shoulders. “Anything is better than sitting on my ass waiting for—” He bit off his words, narrowing his gaze. “Wait. You don’t want me to babysit, do you?”

“Christ, you should be so lucky,” Raphael muttered. “I have an endless mob of females in front of my house just waiting to catch a glimpse of my precious daughter.” He shook his head, not quite capable of disguising his bone-deep pride. “I barely get to hold her unless I steal her from her crib and sneak out of the house.”

“Then what do you want?”

Raphael folded his arms over his chest. "Dr. Young gave us six locations where Stanton Locke might potentially be hiding."

Ah. Now they were getting somewhere.

"You want me to check them out?"

"Actually I've had the adolescent Hunters following up the leads." Raphael grimaced. "They need the practice and they've been itching with the need to do something."

Michel was plagued with the same itch.

Feeling as if he'd been leashed was no doubt a part of the reason he'd become so…consumed with thoughts of Dr. Chelsea Young.

"And?" he asked.

"And I just got a call from Jazz in Bossier City," Raphael said, referring to one of the adolescent Hunters who'd shown great promise. "She's heard rumors that a prominent military contractor recently arrived at Barksdale Air Force Base and set up a secret lab in the abandoned bunkers."

A sick ball of dread lodged in the pit of Michel's gut. Christ. He didn't want to consider the possibility that the human military was somehow involved. It was going to be hard enough to hunt down Locke and stop him without adding in…

No. He gave a sharp shake of his head. He wasn't even going to go there.

Not until they could be sure what was going on.

"What makes her think it has something to do with Locke?" he demanded.

"She thought she caught sight of Locke headed into the base, but lost him in the wetlands that surround the bunkers."

Michel curled his hands into tight fists. Inside, his cat roared with the need to taste blood.

He was going to stop that bastard. One way or another.

"I'll find him," he swore.

Raphael held up a warning hand. "First I want you to discover what his plan is and who's involved."

Michel didn't hesitate. "No problem."

Raphael gave a sharp laugh. "Whatever you lack, Michel, it isn't confidence."

Michel shrugged. He was the best at what he did. False modesty was as ugly as boasting. "You ask, and I deliver."

"True." Raphael paused, a worrisome smile playing around his lips. "But on this occasion you won't have to do it alone."

"A partner?" Michel scowled. What the hell was Raphael thinking? He always worked alone. "That's not really my style."

"It is this time."

Michel stilled, a chill inching down his spine. Something was up. Something he wasn't going to like.

"Who's the lucky Hunter?"

"Not a Hunter."

Michel narrowed his gaze. "A Suit?"

"An expert on Locke."

"Who?" He sucked in a shocked breath as he realized just what his companion was implying. He'd suspected he wasn't going to like what Raphael had to say, but this… "No."

"No?" Raphael's voice was dangerously soft, but Michel was too angry to care.

"You want me to rephrase it?" he snarled. "Hell, no."

Raphael squared his shoulders, his power lashing out like a punch to the gut. Suddenly he was every inch the leader of the Suits.

One badass mofo.

"When I give an order, Michel, it's not up for debate," he stated in tones that defied argument.

He was right.

It was Michel's duty to obey.

Michel glanced toward the sky, a bizarre exhilaration flaring through his body. "Shit."

***

Dr. Chelsea Young was well aware of the two males standing across the small clearing who'd been watching her with the eyes of hungry predators.

She'd have to be dead not to feel the smoldering heat of their gazes. Plus, the injections of Pantera blood she'd given herself over the past six years had heightened her senses to the point she could feel the prickling power of their inner cats.

Of course she was accustomed to Michel's unwavering attention. It didn't matter where she was, or what she was doing. He was always lurking in the background, studying her with a blatant suspicion. She did her best to ignore him. After all, Rage was constantly watching her and she barely noticed him when she was working. But Michel…he disturbed her in a way she couldn't explain.

Maybe it was guilt. God knew she had enough of that to drown in.

Or maybe it was awareness. What woman wouldn't be attracted to his raw, male beauty?

She tensed, acutely aware the two males were moving forward.

Damn.

Hastily she set aside her clipboard and rose to her feet. At the same time she covertly studied the two shifters.

Raphael was the more traditionally handsome, but it was Michel who captivated her attention. His features were chiseled to austere lines that were emphasized by his shaven skull. His eyes were the color of bayou moss, and rimmed with black. They could shimmer with a rare humor, or darken with a lethal fury. His skin was the same coppery shade as his cat when he shifted and his body was layered with slabs of muscles that moved with fluid ease.

Not that she'd been staring. Or ogling. Or sneaking peeks like a creeper.

She swallowed a sigh. *Gah.* There was clearly something wrong with her.

First she'd allowed herself to be seduced by a psychopath who'd eventually held her prisoner. And now she was fascinated by a male who made it painfully clear he wanted her far away from the Wildlands.

Yep. For all her scientific brilliance, she was clearly damaged in the head.

With an effort, she kept her expression one of polite interest as she forced herself to focus on the leader of the Suits.

"Raphael," she said, deliberately ignoring the male who scowled at his side.

"Good morning, Chelsea," Raphael murmured.

A bead of sweat trickled down her back. Despite the chill in the breeze, the Wildlands managed to feel warm and muggy. She told herself it was heat trapped in the thick foliage and the dappled sunlight that fell across her shoulders. Or even the fabric of the loose scrubs she insisted on wearing instead of the pretty sundresses that had been offered to her by the female Pantera.

It couldn't be because she was excited that Michel was standing close enough she could feel his delicious heat wrapping around her.

Because that would be…

Pathetic.

She sucked in a deep breath, ignoring the male musk that saturated the air. "Is there a problem?" she demanded of Raphael.

"I have need of your expertise," the older male murmured.

"Of course," she eagerly agreed. She'd been waiting for an opportunity to go over the studies she'd done on her patients before leaving Benson Enterprises. "I've promised I would do whatever possible to help. Let me get my research notes and—"

"They won't be necessary," Raphael interrupted.

"I don't understand," she said, unconsciously lifting her hand to chew her thumbnail. It was a nervous habit she'd developed after the fire and one she found impossible to break. By the time she went to bed at night, her thumb would be bleeding.

"On this occasion it's your connection to Stanton Locke that can help us."

A sick sense of fear washed through her. Any love she might have felt for Locke was long gone, but she still dreaded the day they came to tell her he was about to be punished for his sins.

"You've captured him?"

Raphael gave a shake of his head. "Not yet, but we believe he's in Bossier City."

She nodded. That was one of the places she'd told them to look for her previous employer.

"I've given you a map to his lab there," she pointed out.

Raphael nodded. "Jazz found the lab and followed a male she believes to be Locke onto the nearby air base."

Okay, she'd done her part. Right?

"What do you want from me?"

"I want you to travel to Bossier City and search through whatever research files we can manage to steal from his lab," Raphael explained. "You'll know what we need to bring back to the Wildlands and what should be turned over to the human authorities."

Ah. That made sense. She gave a nod. "Very well."

"I also want you to discover what his connection is to the human military."

Chelsea hissed in horror. She'd desperately hoped Locke would refuse to give in to Christopher's greed. It was, after all, one thing to use the Pantera blood to try and create a miracle drug that would heal the sick. It was another to use the research to prolong the lives of the rich, or to increase the strength and endurance of soldiers.

A potential threat she hadn't shared with the Pantera.

Along with her other little secret…

"That's impossible," she finally managed to say, her voice thick.

A sudden anger prickled in the air. Michel, of course. Still, it was Raphael who spoke.

"Why?"

She continued to chew her nail, her stomach churning. "If Locke sees me he'll know something is wrong."

"You'll be with Michel," Raphael said in smooth tones. "No one will see you."

With Michel? Was that supposed to be reassuring?

God almighty. She should never have come to the Wildlands. After Locke had released her, she could have fled Louisiana and travelled to Siberia. It might have been cold as hell, but at least no one would bother her and she could forget her past.

"It's too dangerous," she muttered.

Michel abruptly thrust himself into the conversation. "Are you frightened?"

She instinctively bristled. Somehow Michel always rubbed against her nerves.

"Not for myself," she said, her gaze skating over his starkly beautiful face before returning to Raphael. It was too hard to concentrate when the disturbing male was standing so close. "But Locke is ruthless. If he suspects he's been found he'll destroy all evidence of his crimes. Including any—"

She stumbled over the proper word. Naturally, Michel didn't have any trouble offering the most vile suggestions.

"Hostages? Lab rats?" he drawled. "Disposable victims?"

Her gaze remained grimly focused on Raphael. "Patients he might have," she finished.

Raphael nodded, his expression bleak. "It's a risk we have to take."

"Why?" She glanced around the small glade surrounded by towering cypress trees and narrow channels of water. It was as close to paradise as possible on this earth. "You have your people safe."

The two males exchanged a silent glance. There was something they weren't telling her.

At last it was Michel who spoke. "What about the children he created in his Frankenstein lab?" he reminded her. "Don't you imagine that Karen would like to find her sons?"

She flinched. She adored the kindhearted woman who'd treated Chelsea far better than she deserved. The woman had been a breeder and was still looking for two sons who'd been born in Locke's New York labs.

There were few things that she wouldn't do to reunite Karen with her children.

"Of course," she muttered.

"Not to mention the danger if he shared our blood and semen with the military," Raphael piled on. "We have to discover who has access to our DNA."

God. It was so much worse than they even suspected.

She grimaced, biting her tongue. Hopefully they would stop Locke before he could reveal the superpowers of the potent Pantera blood. God only knew what would happen to the Wildlands if the military thought it could provide super-strength to their soldiers.

"Why me?" she demanded.

Raphael studied the flush she knew was staining her cheeks. She had many talents, but lying wasn't one of them.

"You know Locke," he pointed out.

She shrugged. "Not any longer."

The leader of the Suits cocked a brow, not about to let her off so easily.

"You know his preferences in passwords and security. Where he's most likely to hide his most sensitive information," he said. "You'll also be capable of determining what files might help us understand Locke's purpose in Bossier City and how to find Christopher." He paused, holding her wary gaze. "Will you go?"

Like she had a choice?

"Yes," she grudgingly agreed. "But I think it would be better if I went on my own."

Michel took a sharp step forward, crowding into her space as he glared down at her stubborn expression.

"Yeah, I bet you would," he growled. "It would be a perfect opportunity to be reunited with your old friends."

She scowled, but before she could protest there was the soft rustle of grass as Rage abruptly stepped forward.

"Maybe it would be better if I went with her instead of Michel," the young Hunter suggested, his hand lightly touching her shoulder.

Instantly Chelsea felt better. Not because she had fallen victim to Rage's easy charm and stunning beauty.

It was just nice to know that not everyone hated her.

Michel, on the other hand, wasn't at all pleased. His eyes flashed gold as his cat prowled near the surface.

"No," he growled.

Rage frowned. "It's Raph's decision."

Without warning, Michel reached out to grasp her upper arm, yanking her until she was pressed close to his side. Chelsea blinked in surprise. Did he realize what he'd done? Or how possessive it must look to the other males?

She discreetly attempted to tug her arm free, only to have his grip tighten as he continued to glare at Rage.

"This mission needs the skill of a spy, not a Hunter," he said.

Danger prickled in the air as Rage took a step forward. Suddenly the lighthearted flirt was stripped away to reveal the lethal Hunter beneath.

"Not if that spy intends to be a jackass," he countered.

Chelsea held up her hand, the choking heat sizzling between the two males making it difficult for her to breathe.

The last thing she wanted was to cause trouble.

She'd done enough to harm the Pantera.

"It's okay, Rage. This is my..." The word *punishment* hovered on the tip of her tongue before she changed it. No need to provoke the seething male who held onto her like he feared she was about to bolt. "Duty."

CHAPTER 2

Michel wasn't a happy Pantera by the time they arrived in Bossier City.

Not only had he been forced to drive a P.O.S. car instead of his beloved Jag to avoid attracting unwanted attention, but he'd been achingly aware of the female seated next to him.

It didn't matter how hard he tried to ignore her presence; he remained acutely aware of the warm scent of her skin, and the soft sound of her breathing. Worse, his cat had nearly driven him nuts with the urge to lean across the narrow distance and take a small taste.

He didn't trust her. Not even a little.

But he wanted her with a desperation that bordered on obsession.

Shit.

Night had just fallen as they crossed the bridge that spanned the Red River. He flinched at the sound of fighter jets that screamed through the air.

Sometimes heightened senses weren't always a blessing.

Turning onto the parkway that led along the river, he at last found a narrow access road and pulled the car to a halt. Just ahead he could see the small, red-brick building that looked like a factory with tinted windows, steel doors, a narrow parking lot and high, chain-link fence that surrounded the property.

That had to be Locke's secret lab.

Intent on studying the nearby buildings that looked abandoned, Michel was caught off guard when Chelsea abruptly spoke.

"Is there a specific reason I'm receiving the silent treatment or are you always so rude?"

Michel turned in his seat to meet her frustrated glare. *Yes!* He'd been itching for a fight. Anything to distract him from his cock that was hard and aching with a need that truly pissed him off.

"I don't share chitchat with my enemies," he drawled.

Her chin angled to the side, the gesture designed to reveal her displeasure at the same time that she kept her scars hidden by her glorious hair.

Which only pissed him off more.

Did she think the scars distracted from her beauty? If she did, then she was a fool.

"I'm not your enemy," she muttered.

"No?" His lips twisted into a humorless smile. "You didn't experiment on Pantera like they were slabs of meat instead of living, breathing people who suffered unimaginable agony in your labs?"

She paled, as if he'd struck her. "I deeply regret my part in harming your people, as well as the humans who were abused." She turned her head to glance out the window. "I have no excuse."

"Vanity," Michel accused, even as he felt like a total tool.

He didn't know why. Okay, he was being harsh with the female. But she'd helped her cohorts kidnap innocent Pantera as well as humans, including children. Then, without the least amount of mercy, they'd experimented and tormented their victims.

Why should he feel bad because he didn't trust her?

"Yes, it was vanity," she said in low tones, her hands clenched in her lap. "On the other hand, I've tried to do what I can to atone for my mistakes."

His gaze took in the pure lines of her profile before lowering to the slender body that was currently attired in a tight cashmere sweater and jeans that did oh-my-god things to her ass.

He'd almost swallowed his tongue when she'd joined him at the communal garage at the edge of the Wildlands. She was so rarely out of her loose scrubs, he hadn't fully appreciated her sweet curves.

Now he grimly forced his gaze back to her face. Shit. His cock was pressed so tight against his zipper he feared an injury.

"So you claim."

She turned to meet his narrowed gaze. "What's that supposed to mean?"

He shrugged. “It seems convenient that you would have a change of heart just when we managed to discover the Haymore Center and Locke’s sick experiments.”

Her hands clenched in her lap. “There was nothing convenient about it,” she snapped. “I’d been held captive until Locke was forced to cut his losses and leave New Orleans.”

Michel jerked in surprise. He knew that Chelsea had arrived unexpectedly at the Wildlands, and that Raphael and Parish had originally kept her separated from the Pantera. They weren’t going to take any chances with a female who admitted she’d been an employee of their greatest enemy.

After she’d been allowed to join the community, Michel had assumed she’d come straight from one of the labs to the Wildlands. After all, she hadn’t been very forthcoming with her past.

“You were a prisoner?” he demanded.

She gave a jerky nod. “Yes.”

“And they just let you go?”

Her features tightened with pain before she was giving a hesitant nod. “Yes.

Something perilously close to sympathy threatened to undermine the righteous anger he used to keep her at a distance.

No. He couldn’t let down his guard. His duty was to protect his people, not protect this female’s feelings.

“You see?” he sneered. “Convenient.”

Her brows snapped together. “Exactly what are you accusing me of?”

"I think you're a spy," he said without hesitation.

She gave a sharp, disbelieving laugh. "You can't be serious?"

He studied her pale face. Even in the thickening shadows he could make out the delicate lines of her features and the plush temptation of her mouth. Her reaction seemed genuine, but…

"Why wouldn't I be?" he asked.

She snorted. "Because I would make the worst spy in history, that's why."

"That's what you would say, of course."

She heaved a rough sigh. The sort of sigh that women perfected to sound as if they were being tortured beyond bearing.

"If you don't trust me, then why did you agree to bring me to Bossier City?"

"So I can watch you."

Her eyes smoldered with anger. "You seem to watch me a lot."

He tensed. A direct hit.

Barely aware he was moving, he leaned toward the tormenting female, one palm flat on the headrest and the other on the passenger side window.

"I don't trust you."

Astonishingly, she met him glare for glare. She might be quiet, and naturally shy, but she didn't lack courage.

"And that's the only reason?" she taunted.

Deep inside, his cat was suddenly crouched, anxious to pounce on this delicious prey. The animal had enough denying the hunger for this female.

"What do you want me to say?" he demanded, his voice low and husky. "That I've spent my days wondering what you hide beneath those scrubs?" His hand moved from the headrest so his fingers could tangle in her satin hair. "And my nights imagining you spread across my bed?"

Her eyes widened, an unmistakable excitement flaring through the green depths.

"Michel," she breathed.

Her parted lips were a temptation that not even a saint could ignore. And Michel was no saint. He was a frustrated male who hadn't been able to bed a female since he'd caught sight of Dr. Chelsea Young.

Swooping his head down, he crushed her lips in a kiss that was sheer punishment. Or at least, that was his first intention.

But like all best laid plans, the second he felt the soft satin of her mouth, his pressure eased. His anger and suspicion were forgotten as he allowed the tip of his tongue to slip between her lips, exploring her mouth with sensual pleasure. At the same time, his fingers combed through the thick curls, allowing the silken fire to slide over his skin like a caress.

How would it feel to have those curls brushing over his bare chest and down his stomach as she at last took his cock between her lips? Maybe her nails would dig into his ass as he lifted his hips and thrust deep into her mouth, using her tongue to tease the sensitive tip.

The vivid image seared through his mind. He groaned, nearly coming in his jeans when her hands lifted to settle against his chest.

Damn. Chelsea was barely touching him, but it was more exciting than having any other woman do a lap dance.

He gave a gentle tug on her hair, tilting back her head to gain him access to the vulnerable throat. His cat purred in satisfaction, rubbing beneath his skin as his lips skimmed down the line of her jaw before he buried his face against the curve of her neck.

The taste of her slammed into him like a slug to the gut.

Autumn spice and fire.

Intoxicating…

He parted his lips, allowing his teeth to sink into the vulnerable base of her throat. It was only when his cat growled in satisfaction that he realized just how far he was spinning out of control.

"Shit," he muttered, lifting his head to study her, flushed with a seething need.

Clearly lost in her own passion, it took a second for her to lift her lashes and meet his brooding gaze. Then, with an obvious effort, she was placing her hands flat against his chest and giving him a shove.

"Are you out of your mind?" she rasped.

He moved back, not bothering to tell her that her outrage was too little and too late to be convincing.

Right now he was far more concerned with his own painful arousal.

"Obviously," he muttered, reaching to shove open the car door. "Stay here."

Without warning she reached out to grab his arm, her expression troubled. "Where are you going?"

He nodded toward the brick building. "I want to check out the facility."

She released his arm, lifting her hand to chew on her nail. "Locke will have the place surrounded with security," she warned.

"Nothing I can't get past," he said, unconsciously reaching to tug her thumb away from her lips.

It bothered him to see the tip of her thumb raw and bloody from her nervous habit.

She rolled her eyes. "Arrogant," she muttered beneath her breath.

Michel thinned his lips, refusing to allow them to twitch at his unexpected flare of amusement.

"Did you say something?" he mocked.

She met his gaze squarely. "I thought I was sent here to help."

For no reason at all, he felt another surge of lust blast through him. His fingers circled her tiny wrist, his thumb brushing against her fluttering pulse.

"What are you offering?"

Heat smoldered in the air as their gazes locked, and Michel barely battled back the crazed urge to yank her across the seat so she could straddle his lap. He'd never had sex with a woman in a car, let alone when he was parked on a public street. But with this woman he didn't give a shit where they were or who might be watching.

He wanted her.

End of story.

Easily sensing the direction of his thoughts, Chelsea blushed, tugging her arm from his light grip.

"I'm offering my knowledge of Locke's preferences in placing his security cameras and tripwires," she said. "Do you want my help or not?"

"Come on," he muttered, a growl rumbling in his chest as he crawled out of the car and headed down the street.

Another few moments alone with this female and he was going to tell her exactly what he wanted from her.

And it had nothing to do with finding Locke…

***

Stanton Locke should have been impressed. Clearly no expense had been spared to build the vast facility that was spread like a spiderweb beneath the bunkers at the distant edge of the air base.

The labs possessed the latest, high-tech equipment; the rooms for his test subjects were comfortable and yet secure enough to prevent another mass escape like they'd endured just a few weeks before. And there were even startlingly luxurious accommodations for himself and his researchers.

Everything he could want and more.

But while he accepted Benson Enterprises had achieved a new level of success, he was growingly jaded with his master's ambitions.

After all, he understood Christopher's desire to prolong his life. And to discover a way to use the Pantera blood to create a means to heal human diseases. Those were goals that anyone could applaud.

And in the beginning, it'd all been...morally acceptable, if not entirely legal.

The Pantera had struggled with becoming pregnant, and Christopher had dedicated himself to providing the solution to their problem. At first he'd used the old-fashioned method of sharing his seed with the females desperate for a child. Then, once he realized the Pantera's potent blood could not only heal the hideous scars that had been left from the smallpox he'd survived as a child, but also prolong his life, he'd invested his considerable fortune in trying to find a clinical means of creating more Pantera.

Christopher's investment had included collecting the finest scientific minds he could hire and giving them carte blanche to experiment on the various Pantera and humans he captured and kept locked in his various labs.

Slowly, however, his master's offer to help the Pantera got twisted with a determination to create a variety of serums that would offer everything from super-strength to curing cancer to potential immortality.

Why not make a profit on his investment?

But Locke had never dreamed Christopher would cross the threshold into making their experiment subjects into 'mutant' soldiers.

Now he was sinking in shit so deep he didn't know how to get out.

Walking down the long corridor that was painfully bright from the overhead fluorescent lights, Locke took a brief moment to appreciate the knowledge that Chelsea was at least free. He'd done many things in his life that shamed him.

But releasing the only woman he'd ever loved…

Well, that was one choice that allowed him to sleep at night.

Stepping into his large personal office that was furnished with a solid oak desk and matching chairs, he barely resisted the urge to reach for the handgun he had holstered beneath the jacket of his gray Armani suit.

The large, bald-headed man standing in the center of the office was the sort of male who inspired fear.

It wasn't just his thick body that bulged with muscles beneath the crisply pressed uniform. Or the heavily-jowled face that held an expression of sneering superiority. It was the watery blue eyes that were as flat as a snake.

This was a man without mercy. Or empathy.

A man trained to be the perfect killing machine.

And now he was the largest defense contractor in the world.

"Colonel Cole."

The older man ran a cold glance over Locke's designer suit before returning to take in the dark hair he kept smoothed into a tail at his nape. Cole made an effort to hide his disdain for Locke's elegant style and polished English accent, but he was one of those overzealous patriots who never truly trusted anyone stupid enough not to be born in America.

The man forced a smile to his lips. Locke suppressed a shudder. It looked like the man had *rigor mortis*.

"I've told you, my name is Richard," he insisted.

"Richard." Locke offered an equally forced smile. The Colonel would be truly horrified if he knew that beneath Locke's sophistication was a filthy street urchin who'd been pulled out of the London gutters. "I didn't expect you until next week."

The older man waved his beefy hand toward the door. "I wanted to make sure the facilities meet your approval."

Locke shrugged. He'd argued long and hard with Christopher to remain in his old labs. Once they moved into this lab built by Cole Security and owned by the military, then they would no longer be in control of their own experiments.

They would have a dozen people looking over their shoulders, telling them what to do, how to do it, and when to do it.

Unfortunately, Christopher had reminded him that over the past months they'd become increasingly vulnerable. Not only to the furious Pantera, but to government agencies who weren't nearly so forgiving of their…less-than-legal operations.

Besides, Cole Security was paying them a lot of money.

"They are state of the art," he murmured, moving to lean against the edge of his desk.

A subtle reminder that this was *his* office.

The smile disappeared to reveal the ruthless man who'd been quietly asked to retire from the air force after it was discovered he'd nearly beaten one of his officers to death over a card game.

"Then, no complaints?"

"Did you assume there would be?" Locke demanded, careful to keep his face wiped of expression.

"I did hear word that you haven't resumed your…" Richard paused to choose his words with care. "Procedures. Naturally I feared there might be a problem."

Locke shrugged. There was no way in hell he could admit that he'd been doing his best to stall for time. He didn't know why, or what he hoped to achieve. He just knew he had a very bad feeling about turning over Pantera blood to the Colonel and his cronies.

"The test subjects have been moved on several occasions over the past month," he pointed out, his fingers giving his French cuffs a small tug. "Their adrenaline levels will be elevated and their immune systems depressed. I prefer to give them a few days to settle in."

The muscles in Richard's thick neck bulged as he struggled to contain his temper. "How many days?"

"Four, maybe five."

"That's unfortunate." The drawled words held an unmistakable threat. "You promised me the lab would be up and running a week ago."

"It was." Locke shrugged. "My lab was prepared, and then you insisted we move into these facilities."

The Colonel waved aside his logic. "It's far more secure. And it was hardly a move. It's less than two miles from your lab."

Locke thinned his lip. Bloody hell. He hated dealing with idiots.

"These are live test subjects, not pieces of steel on an assembly line," he managed to say without revealing his inner aversion. "It's deeply unsettling for them to be taken from a place they've become accustomed to and moved to new surroundings. It doesn't matter if it's a mile or a thousand miles."

Richard's face flushed to an ugly shade of puce, his hand deliberately moving to the gun that was holstered at his side.

"And I'm dealing with stockholders who expect a profit on the considerable investment we made in your employer," he bit out. "Each day that passes without progress is day they're losing money. And I can assure you they don't like losing money."

Damn. Locke swallowed a sigh. It was obvious he'd procrastinated as long as he dared.

He wasn't afraid of Colonel Richard Cole. The puffed-up blowhard might think he was tough, but he'd never come upon a man who'd spent the first years of his life struggling to survive.

But he didn't want to alert Christopher to the fact that he'd been dragging his feet. His master wouldn't be amused.

"I'll try to resume my work tomorrow," he grudgingly promised.

Of course the prick couldn't just be satisfied with that.

"When can I expect to share your efforts with my prospective buyers?" he pressed.

"I can't give you an exact time."

"Then let me do it for you." The Colonel moved forward to point a blunt finger directly in Locke's face. "I'll pick you up on Thursday afternoon. Make sure you're prepared to impress."

With a precise, military turn, Richard was heading toward the door, his heels clicking on the floor.

Left on his own, Locke moved to open the bottom drawer of his desk, pulling out the twenty-year-old bottle of cognac. After being abandoned by his alcoholic mother, he rarely touched spirits. But if ever a time demanded a drink…this was it.

"Bloody hell," he muttered, pouring a shot and tossing it down his throat.

CHAPTER 3

Michel had never considered himself a male who could be led around by his cock.

Just the opposite.

He was a male who had a firm leash on his impulses. And passions.

The early years of being forced to watch the world from his bedroom window had taught him patience, grim determination, and overall self-discipline.

So why did he turn into some raving sex addict the second he caught this female's scent?

Refusing to contemplate the most obvious explanation, he halted behind an empty Dumpster and studied the brick building.

"Give me the rundown," he said in clipped tones.

Chelsea stood at his side, but with several inches separating them. Because she feared he might try to kiss her again? Or because she was as conscious as he was of the heat smoldering between them?

"He'll have cameras at each corner of the roof." She pointed toward the recently replaced eaves where he could see a small camera. "He'll also have the fence wired to sound an internal alarm whenever anything touches it."

Michel nodded, his gaze taking in the empty parking lot and the darkened windows. The place felt…empty.

"Guards?"

"It's hard to say," she said, her voice so soft only a Pantera could pick up the words.

With a frown he turned his head to study her profile. "Why?"

"Because I don't know how many he brought with him." She shrugged. "If he's planning to make this his base he'll have two dozen guards. If it's a temporary hideout then he'll only have three or four."

"Anything else you can tell me?"

"Yes, I sense…" She hesitated, gnawing her nail as she gazed toward the dark building.

He absently reached to tug her thumb away from her mouth, studying her distracted expression.

"What do you sense?"

"A human, maybe two." She paused, then gave a shake of her head. "No Pantera."

Michel gave a slow nod, his gaze continuing to search for hidden dangers. Despite his cat's strange belief in the female standing next to him, he would be a fool not to suspect this was a trap.

"I'm going to do a quick sweep," he abruptly decided, sending her a warning frown. "Don't move."

She blinked in surprise. "How are you going to—"

She bit off her words as he easily vaulted onto the edge of the Dumpster and bounded onto a nearby tree. From there it was easy to find a branch high enough to allow him to jump over the fence without setting off the alarms.

Landing lightly, he crouched down and listened. When he was certain there was nothing to hear but the sound of Chelsea's breathing, he rose to his feet and darted along the edge of the parking lot. He couldn't completely avoid the camera, but he moved faster than a human. If someone was monitoring the area they would see nothing more than a dark blur.

Circling to the back, he caught sight of a black van that was pulled up to an open loading dock. He could smell human males, but he didn't pause to investigate. Instead he continued his sweep of the property. Only when he reached the front of the building did he move forward to enter the basement through a narrow window.

Discovering himself in a long room filled with cages, his inner cat growled at the unmistakable scent of Pantera in the air.

His people had been held captive in this basement. And not long ago.

Pausing at the nearest cage he bent down, drawing in a deep breath.

Pantera. Humans. And something else.

But Chelsea was right. They'd left at least two days before.

He checked out another long room filled with cages and then busted through a locked door at the very end of the basement. As he hoped, inside was the security office with stacks of monitors and a computer that ran the alarm system.

With an expertise that had made him such a successful spy, he disabled every alarm and shut down the cameras. Then, confident that no one could track him, he moved through the upper floors.

It swiftly became obvious that Locke had left in a hurry with his prisoners and most of his staff. And that he wasn't planning on coming back. At least, not any time soon. The stainless steel labs were eerily empty and the offices stripped of any personal items, including computers and files.

Completing his search, Michel headed toward the back of the building where he could smell the two humans. With a peek around the corner to make sure he wouldn't be noticed, he entered the loading dock, sliding silently through the darkness to study the men as they moved crates into the back of the van.

Both were large and dressed in green uniforms. One, however, had gray hair that was clipped short and the other had long, shaggy black hair that he kept shoving from his petulant face as he loaded another box.

"This is bullshit," the younger man complained, turning to glare at the gray-haired guard who was clearly there to supervise. "We just unpacked all this shit last week. Now we have to move it all a couple miles down the road. Why didn't we take it there in the first place?"

His companion shrugged, studying the clipboard in his hands. "You're new, so I'm going to give you one warning," he drawled. "Asking questions in this job is a good way to end up dead. You want to live, then you do what you're told and keep your mouth shut."

The younger man shrugged, moving toward another crate. "It's just the two of us. All the nerds left with the animals."

Michel stilled, his instincts on full alert. They were discussing the Pantera.

"Yeah well, the walls have ears."

The younger guard abruptly straightened, his broad face twisting with an expression of horror.

"Shit. We're being bugged?"

"Do you want to take the chance?"

Even from a distance, Michel could see the man shudder.

Locke obviously led his gang of thugs with fear. Not surprising. There was no way he could have kept his gruesome experimentations a secret if he hadn't made sure his employees were terrified to reveal his secrets.

"Hell no," the guard muttered.

"Then shut up and work," the older man ordered, waving his hand toward the stacks of crates still waiting to be loaded. "I want a few hours of shuteye before the driver arrives to take this last load to Mr. Locke."

The younger guard grunted as he picked up a crate and headed toward the van. "What time is he supposed to be here?"

The gray-haired man checked his clipboard. "Eight a.m. sharp."

Michel smiled. So. A driver was going to take the van to Locke.

How convenient.

A smile of anticipation curled his lips. The sight would have caused the two humans to piss their pants if they'd seen it. Unfortunately for them, they didn't even know they were in danger before Michel had pounced, knocking them both senseless with more force than necessary. Then, dumping them into an open crate, he put the lid on top and nailed it shut.

Hey, it seemed fitting.

Pausing long enough to call for a local Hunter to come and pick up the unconscious men, Michel jumped out of the loading bay and hurried to the side of the building where he'd left Chelsea waiting.

A strange warmth spread through him at the sight of her crouched behind the Dumpster, a worried expression tightening her pretty features.

She'd waited.

Breaking the lock on the narrow gate, he gestured her forward, instinctively wrapping his fingers around her wrist to tug her thumb away from her mouth as she halted at his side.

"Is Locke there?" she demanded.

"No." He frowned. There was something in her voice…something he couldn't put his finger on. "There were two goons packing up a bunch of files."

She grimaced, smart enough to know that he hadn't just walked away from them. "Are they…?"

"Dead?" He shook his head. "No. I locked them in a crate and called a Hunter to pick them up and take them to the Wildlands. They might have information we need."

She glanced down to where his fingers were absently running a path up and down the satin skin of her inner arm.

"What do you want from me?"

He jerked away his hand, feeling as if he'd been scalded. Since when did he touch her like they were lovers?

"I'm going to finish loading the crates in the van," he said in clipped tones. "I want you to go through the offices and make sure nothing's been overlooked. The guards didn't look overly bright."

She gave a jerky nod, her face flushed. "Fine."

Leading her to the front of the building, he busted open the door to urge her to the upper floor. During his earlier sweep, he'd noticed there was a private apartment he assumed belonged to Locke.

He waited at the doorway as she entered the front room that had been converted to an office. On the point of joining her, he was halted as his phone vibrated. Pulling it out of his pocket, he glanced at the screen.

"The Hunter is here," he murmured. "I need to meet him in the loading dock."

"Okay," Chelsea murmured, her expression distracted as if she was considering where she wanted to start the search.

"I won't be long."

She was headed toward the desk when he was jogging back down the stairs and into the dock to help the Hunter load the crate with the guards, along with all the other boxes, into the back of his truck. Once he was sure nothing had been overlooked, he commanded the Hunter to drive non-stop to the Wildlands.

He paused to lock the van and shut the doors to the loading dock. He intended to have a little surprise for the driver when he arrived in the morning. But for now, they needed to finish their search and get some sleep.

Turning off the lights, he moved through the empty building. He could see perfectly in the dark, but he didn't need his heightened vision to be able to find Chelsea.

Her scent tugged at his senses until he was fairly certain he could have found her if she was hiding on the other side of the world. Knowledge that was more than a little disturbing.

***

Chelsea fiercely concentrated on the files she'd managed to discover locked in a safe that had been hidden in the floor. They were heavily encrypted and so far all she'd managed to figure out was that they referred to some secret sect of Pantera and the Everglades.

Her concentration, however, couldn't block out the rich scent of male musk that filled the air as Michel climbed the stairs and entered the apartment. She instinctively stiffened, then, as he headed directly into the bedroom, she breathed out a sigh of relief.

Gah. She'd known this was going to be unpleasant.

Being trapped with a person who could barely disguise their hatred for you was never fun. But she hadn't been expecting the ruthless arousal that pulsed between them, rubbing her nerves raw.

And now that he'd kissed her…

The awareness she'd always experienced since catching sight of the mysterious spy had intensified into something a thousand times more annoying. She felt restless. On edge. As if there was a need vibrating deep inside her that was about to explode. She'd never experienced anything like it before.

It would be easy to tell herself that it was a reaction to the Pantera blood she'd injected over the years. It might very well be setting off some strange mating urge now that she was staying in the Wildlands.

A damned shame the reasonable theory didn't explain why only Michel seemed to inspire the intense reaction.

Still rifling through the files, she was brooding on her unwelcomed hunger for a male who considered her the enemy when there was the sound of approaching footsteps and Michel's rough voice sliced through the air.

"What the hell?"

With a jolt of alarm, Chelsea dropped the files and rose to her feet. "What's wrong?"

Striding grimly forward, Michel held out a small picture frame he'd obviously discovered in the bedroom.

"Do you want to explain this?"

She didn't need to look at the photo he was waving beneath her nose. She knew it was an image of herself standing beside a lake with Locke at her side. They were gazing at each other and smiling. Two people who were clearly intimately familiar with each other.

Crap.

"It's a photo," she muttered.

A growl rumbled in his chest, his eyes flashing gold. "Don't push me."

Without warning, he threw the picture across the room, as if it somehow offended him.

And maybe it did. She'd always known she was taking a risk in not revealing she'd been Locke's lover. But…

She hunched her shoulders, absently chewing her thumbnail. "What do you want to know?"

"Why does Locke have a picture of the two of you together?"

She glanced toward the broken frame and glass that was shattered over the floor. "I've never hidden the fact we worked closely together."

"How close?" Wrapping his fingers around her wrist he pulled her hand away from her mouth in a growingly familiar habit. Then, when she refused to answer, he tightened his grip and tugged her until she was pressed against his chest. "Dr. Young?"

Tilting back her head, she sucked in a sharp breath as she met his smoldering gaze. His cat was studying her with an intensity that made the hairs on her nape stand upright.

"That's none of your business."

He leaned down until they were nose to nose. "How close?"

She shivered. Even as he glared at her in furious suspicion, she couldn't halt her feminine reaction to the feel of her breasts pressed against his hard muscles.

Clearly she was demented.

"Dammit," she breathed.

"Tell me," he commanded, his voice a low growl.

Chelsea heaved a resigned sigh. "Very close."

"You were lovers."

"Yes."

Without warning he released her wrist and stepped back to study her with a scowl.

"You didn't think you should share that little tidbit of information?"

She absently rubbed her wrist. Not because it hurt. For all his suspicions, Michel had always touched her with a surprising tenderness. But she could still feel the heat of his touch scalding her skin.

"No." She gave a lift of her shoulder. "Like I said, it's none of your business."

His jaw clenched, the air pulsing with the force of his anger. "We both know that's a lie. Your relationship with Locke is very much my business."

She tilted her chin, not even caring that her scars were showing. "Why?"

He clenched his hands. "Because it proves you have every reason to betray us."

"You assume everything proves I have reason to betray you," she accused, suddenly tired of playing the role of villain. Had she made bad choices? Yes. Had she trusted the wrong people? Yes. But she'd been punished and now she was doing everything in her power to repair the damage she'd caused. Enough was enough. "What do I have to do to prove I'm no longer working for my previous employers?"

He pointed toward the shattered picture. "Tell me the truth."

She gave a grudging nod. "Fine, but not here."

There was a long pause before he moved to scoop the stack of files she'd discovered off the floor.

"Are you finished?" he inquired, his voice oddly flat.

She glanced around the office. She'd searched everywhere she could imagine Locke would have stashed his private files.

"I've found everything I'm going to."

"Let's go."

In a tense silence they left the building and returned to Michel's car. The silence lingered as they drove a few blocks and halted in front of a small house surrounded by a high fence. Pulling out his phone, Michel punched in a number and seconds later a gate slid open. He gunned the engine to pull up a short drive and directly into the open garage bay.

Barely glancing in her direction, Michel shut off the engine and crawled out of the car. Chelsea sighed, hurriedly moving to join him as he walked to the side of the garage and placed his hand on a small scanner that was designed to read his prints.

She got that he was pissed. She should have revealed she'd been intimately involved with Locke.

But, yeesh.

The prickling heat that was filling the air threatened to choke her.

"What is this place?" Chelsea inquired, her brows lifting as a hidden door glided open and Michel stepped into the short tunnel that led into the attached building.

"This is the closest safe house," he said, leading her through a small but ruthlessly clean kitchen and equally tidy living room that was decorated with flowered sofas and tables filled with knickknacks.

Anyone glancing through the window would assume it was the home of a traditional granny. Chelsea, however, didn't miss the cameras tucked in the corners of the ceiling and the steel shutters that could be closed to keep out an intruder.

Michel continued his swift pace into the hallway and up a narrow flight of stairs. It wasn't until they were in the bedroom at the very back of the house that he at last halted so he could turn to face her.

Chelsea glanced around, taking in the wide double bed covered by a handmade quilt, and the sturdy walnut furnishings. It was…homey. A sudden weariness flared through Chelsea.

She wanted nothing more than to crawl onto that bed and tumble into a deep, dreamless sleep.

"Is this my room?" she demanded.

"It is." Michel stabbed her with a threatening glare. "I'll warn you now that the phones are tapped and there's no way to get in or out unless I unlock the doors."

Her lips thinned, and she barely resisted the urge to punch him in the junk. "You're wearing on my nerves," she rasped.

"The feeling is mutual."

She met him glare for glare, trying to ignore the tiny shivers racing through her body.

"Now what?" she challenged. "Handcuffs and whips?"

The hint of gold in his eyes abruptly deepened as his anger transformed into something far more dangerous.

Stepping forward, he deliberately wrapped her in the thunderous power that radiated around his hard, muscular body.

"Now there's a thought." His voice was husky, filled with hunger that echoed deep inside her. "I'm sure I could find any bedroom toys you might need to turn you on."

Her mouth went dry, her pussy clenching at the thought of being handcuffed to the bed while this male stripped off her clothes.

Would he be quick or slow?

Would he want to torment her by licking and stroking down her quivering form? Or would he take her with a swift fury that would leave them both aching from pleasure?

And what did he mean by *bedroom toys*?

A strangled groan was wrenched from her throat as she tried to squash the treacherous images searing through her brain. What was wrong with her?

"I meant, do you intend to beat the truth out of me?" She forced the words past her stiff lips.

He hissed, as if offended by her question. Then his jaw tightened.

"I could torture you like you did to Reny and Sév and a hundred other Pantera," he accused.

"Don't," she breathed, not bothering to explain she'd never been involved in torturing anyone.

Whether she'd personally caused the patients pain or not, she'd been a part of Benson Enterprises. That made her guilty by association.

"Then explain," he snapped.

Stepping back, she wrapped her arms around her waist. She hated talking about the past.

It dredged up all the pain and guilt that stained her soul like a cancer.

"I was thirteen when our house caught on fire and burned to the ground," she said, grimacing at the memory of acrid smoke that had blanketed her bedroom, waking her in the middle of the night. "When I heard the alarm I tried to find my parents and younger brother, but the flames were too intense." She touched the scars that marred her face. The agony of her burns had taken months to fade. "Eventually I jumped out my bedroom window."

She thought she heard Michel suck in a startled breath. "They died?"

"Yes." She kept her gaze averted, feeling painfully vulnerable. "I went to live with my grandmother, but it wasn't easy." She gave a humorless laugh. That was the understatement of the century. Her grandmother could barely stand to look at her, and enduring the horror of her classmates…yeah, not fun. "Not only did the scars make me different from the other students, but they were a constant reminder to my grandmother of her loss." She shrugged. "I had a crazy idea that if I could erase the scars I could somehow erase the pain."

Michel moved toward her, but thankfully, he didn't try to touch her. She didn't think she could concentrate if she was battling her intense reaction to him.

"That's why you agreed to help Locke," he murmured.

She nodded. "He approached me after I published a paper on my research in genetic engineering. He promised me the sort of funding I could only dream of."

"And it didn't bother you when you discovered he was holding innocent people captive for your experiments?"

She hunched her shoulders, knowing that he would never understand. Not just her desperation to heal her face, but to satisfy her scientific curiosity.

The mere thought that she could create an antidote that could help heal almost any wound or disease was intoxicating.

"At first I had no idea where the blood came from," she admitted, unable to believe how naive she'd been. "Then when I eventually learned the truth I was so close to a breakthrough that I didn't let myself consider who was being hurt."

He made a sound of disgust. "The end justified the means?"

"Something like that."

"And you were in love with Locke?" he accused.

There was a strange edge in his voice that made her at last lift her head to meet his smoldering gaze.

"No." She shook her head. "I was in love with the man he might have been if he could have walked away from his master."

The cat was briefly visible in his eyes. Watchful. Hungry.

Then the male regained control.

"You mean Christopher?"

"Yes." She'd already shared all the information she had on Christopher, although it wasn't much.

"Why did they make you a prisoner?"

She blinked at the unexpected question. She didn't think he cared why she'd been voted off the island.

"I tried to leave."

His expression was stripped of all emotion, his body clenched with a tension that hummed in the air.

"Why?"

"It wasn't one thing," she admitted. "It wasn't just a growing realization of how many lives were being destroyed." She started to lift her hand only to drop it when he instantly reached out, as if to prevent her thumb from reaching her teeth. This male might very well break her childhood habit. Or, more likely, drive her to drink. "And a fear."

"A fear of what?"

"Of what they intended to do with my research," she said. She wrinkled her nose. Her fights with Locke had been epic when she'd tried to destroy the computer files that held her research. "I tried to convince Locke that things were spiraling out of control, but he refused to listen." She shrugged. "So I decided it was time to quit."

His gaze narrowed. "That's when they imprisoned you?"

"No." Her features tightened. "There was only one way out of the organization, according to Christopher."

He frowned in confusion as he easily realized what she was implying. "You said you were a prisoner."

"I was. Locke faked my death and hid me in a house in New Orleans, complete with locks and a guard."

He gave a slow nod, his expression still impossible to read. "You escaped?"

"No, he released me before he fled."

"Why?"

"He claimed he still had feelings for me," she said with blunt honesty. If she was caught in another lie, she knew beyond a doubt this male would never forgive her. "But I can't be certain that he didn't expect me to do exactly what I did. Run to the Wildlands."

CHAPTER 4

Michel studied her pale face, the last of his resistance crumbling beneath the stark revelations.

Raphael had been right. Dammit. What he was feeling was more than sympathy. He truly did understand her pain. He'd suffered the same knowledge he was different from others.

Unlike Chelsea, however, he hadn't been alone.

During his darkest days, he'd had a loving family and pack who'd supported him. Without them he might very well have turned out to be a bitter recluse who cursed a fate that had left him crippled.

"Do you believe me?" She interrupted his dark brooding, her expression defensive.

Michel heaved a deep sigh before giving a grudging nod of his head. "Yes."

"Well, don't leap for joy," she muttered. "You might hurt yourself."

He lifted a hand to rub the short stubble of his hair. He could continue to act like an ass, or he could admit the truth. It was the way she squared her shoulders, as if preparing for one of his scathing retorts, that made his decision for him.

Shit. He'd done enough damage.

More than enough.

"It's…" He struggled for the words to explain his behavior.

"Complicated?" she mocked.

A humorless laugh was wrenched from his throat. She had no idea.

"When I first caught sight of you I was stunned," he told her.

She wrinkled her nose. "You made it clear what you thought of me."

"No, I didn't." He held her gaze. Odd. He'd assumed his pride would take a beating at his confession. Instead he felt nothing but a surge of relief. "Not even to myself."

"What do you mean?"

"I saw you only hours after you arrived. I was dazzled by your beauty." He frowned as she reached to cover her scars. Stepping forward, he brushed aside her fingers so he could frame her face with his hands. "Stop," he commanded in stern tones. You're beautiful. A few scars will never change that."

Her eyes widened, a heartbreaking vulnerability shimmering in the emerald depths.

"You hate me."

He flinched. Her words felt like a knife slicing through him.

"As I said, I saw you and I felt like I'd been hit by a truck," he insisted, his cat purring as the scent of autumn spice saturated the air around him. "Then Raphael told me you'd been working for Locke. I was—"

"Furious," she interrupted.

"And thankful."

She blinked in confusion. "Thankful?"

He grimaced. "It gave me the perfect excuse to fight my attraction to you."

There was a long pause as she studied his expression. What was she searching for?

"And that was important?" she at last demanded.

"Yes."

Her lips flattened with annoyance. "Because I'm connected to Locke or because I'm human?"

Ah. If only it was so simple.

"Neither. I wanted to fight my attraction because it was too powerful," he bluntly admitted. "I didn't like feeling that my emotions were spinning out of control."

She sucked in a sharp breath, an unexpected hurt darkening her eyes. "Is this some sort of sick game you're playing with me?"

"Hell no," he instantly growled, lowering his head until he could brush his lips over her scarred cheek. "I'll admit I'm a master at playing games, but this is all too serious."

She stiffened, her fingers curling around his wrists as she tried to pull away.

"Michel, don't," she pleaded.

He lifted his head. For an agonizing minute he thought she was rejecting his touch. Not that he didn't deserve it. But damn, he was just now accepting how desperately he needed this female.

It couldn't be too late.

Then he abruptly realized she was protesting his kiss against her scars.

His brows drew together as he scowled down at her wary expression.

"It wasn't your fault that you survived."

"I know, it's just…" She made another bid for freedom. "They're ugly."

Michel lowered his head, once again pressing his lips to her cheek. "Not to me."

"Right," she muttered.

He nuzzled a path to the curve of her ear. "You don't believe me?"

She trembled. "No."

Michel knew how he wanted to convince her that he found her profoundly and utterly enchanting. Scars and all.

But he forced himself to pull back. He wanted to make damned sure she understood that there was nothing that could make her anything less than beautiful to him.

"Then let me show you," he said, stepping back to pull off his boots before straightening to undo his zipper.

"What are you doing?" She gave a small gasp as he shoved down his jeans and stepped out of them, revealing his preference for going commando. But even as her cheeks heated with a combination of embarrassment and unmistakable arousal, her gaze drifted down to take in the deep scars that ran along the outside of his thighs to mid-calf on each leg. She lifted her head in confusion. "What happened?"

"I had a birth defect that left me lame when I was a cub," he explained. "It wasn't until human technology progressed enough to replace my joints that I was able to walk."

"Oh." Her tension melted as her scientific curiosity kicked into gear. Bending down, she studied the thick scars that marred his dark skin. "I thought Pantera healed too fast to leave blemishes?"

He gave a low growl, his cock hardening. Did she have any idea what X-rated fantasies she was inspiring as she bent toward him?

If she didn't, she was going to find out.

Very, very soon.

"My body tried to reject the metal alloy in the knee joint," he said, his voice thickening with his growing need. "It kept me from healing for weeks."

She straightened, a flush touching her cheeks. Clearly she'd had enough Pantera blood to catch the scent of his arousal.

Or maybe it was his fully erect cock that was giving him away.

She took a step backward. Like that was going to ease the passion that was smoking between them.

"What happens when you shift?"

He stepped forward, not about to give her space.

"My cat absorbs the new material. But the scars remain." He held her gaze. "Do they offend you?"

"Of course not."

"Why not?" He moved even closer, sucking in a deep breath of her feminine scent. The air heated with his cat's hunger. "They're a symbol of my weakness."

"No," she breathed, her hand automatically lifting so she could chew her nail. "They represent your strength."

"Just as yours represent the miracle of life." He grabbed her hand, pulling it to his lips. Her grandmother had made her feel as if her life represented failure. He intended to make her realize it was a triumph. "You survived, Chelsea. That should be celebrated."

She released a slow, shaken breath, her heart thundering loud enough for him to pick up the rapid beat.

"You confuse me," she whispered.

Releasing her hand, he tugged his sweatshirt over his head and tossed it aside. "The feeling is mutual," he assured her, a smile curving his lips as her gaze took in his bare chest, lingering on his puma tattoo.

She licked her lips.

Was she thinking about tasting him?

Hell, he hoped so.

"Then why are you doing this?" she demanded.

"This?"

Without warning, Michel leaned down to scoop her off her feet. He'd been achingly aware of the nearby bed from the moment they'd entered the room. Now he intended to make full use of it.

"Michel," she breathed in shock. But she made no effort to escape.

Thank the Goddess. She was stronger than a normal human, but he was still far more powerful. If she even hinted that she was uncomfortable with his touch he would have to back away.

And he didn't want to back away.

"Christ, I like to hear you say my name," he murmured, his gaze locked on her face as he watched every emotion flick over her delicate features.

Wariness. Excitement. And a hunger that matched his own.

"Tell me why."

He gently laid her in the center of the mattress. "I'm doing this because if I don't have you soon I think I'm going to combust," he said with a simple honesty.

Slowly her gaze swept over his body, lingering on his cock that hardened at the scent of her arousal that whispered through the air.

Autumn spice. His mouth watered for a taste.

"You can do more than look, Dr. Young," he breathed, lowering himself to stretch beside her, his cat preening beneath her heated gaze. "You can touch."

Her lips twitched with a hint of amusement. "How generous."

"Well, I'm a generous kind of cat." He shocked himself by teasing. He wasn't a playful cat. Or at least he'd never been before tonight. But with this female… Holding her gaze, he reached for her hand to press it against his aching dick. "Feel what you do to me."

"Michel."

She hesitated, then perhaps reading the fierce need in his eyes, she gently allowed her fingers to curl around his cock. He sucked in a sharp breath as she skimmed up to trace the broad tip. *Holy shit.* His balls were already tight, his seed poised to explode.

He was threatening to come just from her light touch.

A slow smile curved her lips as she studied his rigid features and the bead of sweat that trickled down his bare chest. The beautiful tease was clearly enjoying his torment.

He shuddered, sitting up to swiftly rid her of her clothing. If they'd been in the Wildlands he would have simply exposed his claws and shredded them away. Now he cursed every second that was wasted wiggling her out of her jeans and sweater.

Once he had her naked, he paused long enough to admire her slender form. Christ. Her hair was a cascade of fire as it trailed over the pillow, her eyes shimmering like pale emeralds, her body drenched silver in the moonlight.

Exquisite.

Unable to resist temptation, he reached to trail his fingers over her wide brow and down the slender length of her nose.

"I know I'm rushing you," he admitted in rough tones. "But I've waited too long to have you." He released a shaken sigh, his fingers moving to deliberately brush over the scars that roughened her cheek. “It’s killing me.”

She stiffened, but thankfully didn’t pull away from his tender caress. Michel felt a fierce surge of pleasure. He was honored by her trust. He, better than anyone, understood just how difficult it was for her not to jerk away.

“Are you going to regret this in the morning?”

He grimaced, knowing what she was asking.

She feared he was going to return to being the cold, distant male who’d tried so hard to pretend he wasn’t completely fascinated by her.

“The only thing I regret is punishing you because I was afraid of being vulnerable,” he growled, his hand moving down the curve of her neck. “I was a jackass.”

“Yes. You were.” She gave his cock a slow pump, her fingers hitting his sensitive balls with fucking perfection. Damn. “But I still wanted you.”

“Thank the Goddess,” he breathed, groaning as she gave another pump. Gently he removed her fingers from his cock, knowing another squeeze and he was going to blow. “I might not deserve your desire, but I intend to take full advantage of it.”

“Maybe I’m taking advantage of you,” she warned, a tiny smile curving her lips and making his heart squeeze with a sharp regret.

Why hadn’t he been doing everything in his power to earn that lovely smile? Because he was a stubborn idiot, that was why.

“Feel free to take advantage whenever, wherever, and as much as you want,” he murmured in throaty tones, his fingers lowering to cup the magnificent swell of her breast.

"You mean for tonight?" she kept her tone light, as if his answer didn't matter.

Michel's cat growled. One night was never going to be enough. Hell, he wasn't sure he could *ever* have enough.

"For as long as you'll allow me to be a part of your life," he said, delighted when he heard her heartbeat skip at his low words.

"I…" Her words trailed away as he lowered his head to capture the tip of her breast between his lips. Using his tongue, he teased her nipple until it was a tight bud and she was squirming beneath him. "Oh my god," she moaned.

"Can we begin again, Chelsea?" he entreated, taking time to pleasure her other nipple before he trailed tiny kisses in the valley between her breasts.

She hesitated, still hurting from his cutting suspicion, before she heaved a soft sigh.

"Everyone deserves a second chance," she whispered.

His lips skimmed over the soft swell of her belly. "Thank you," he rasped, relief flooding through him.

He didn't know where this was going, but he knew he couldn't bear to live with the knowledge he'd irrevocably damaged the possibilities that hovered between them.

Continuing to head toward her sweet spot, Michel was caught off guard when his lips brushed the tiny diamond that pierced her belly button.

So, his starchy doctor had a whimsical side. His cat stroked against the inside of his skin, pleased with the sparkling bit of jewelry. Maybe together they could learn to enjoy the present without allowing the past to cast shadows.

Rubbing his nose against her satin skin, he teased the tiny diamond with the tip of his tongue.

She squirmed in delight. "That tickles," she breathed.

He smiled with satisfaction. "I'll be back to play with that later," he promised.

For now he had other treasures to discover.

"When do I get to play?"

The sweet aroma of her arousal filled the air, luring him ever downward.

"Later," he husked. "Much, much later."

"Not fair," she muttered, but her legs readily parted to allow him to settle between them.

Sliding his arms under her thighs, he effectively pinned her to the mattress as he spread her wide enough to give him a perfect view of her luscious pussy.

Yes. He gave a throaty sigh, leaning forward to lap through her rich cream.

Decadent pleasure shuddered through him.

This female was everything he'd ever wanted.

Strong, intelligent, capable of compassion and dedicated to helping those she'd hurt in the past.

And sexy as hell.

Continuing to run his tongue over her swollen clit, he savored the taste of autumn spice that made his cat shudder with pleasure. His tongue dipped into her body, surging in and out until she was panting with need.

"Michel, please," she pleaded in thick tones.

With one last lingering taste, he slid up her body, hissing at the electricity that sparked between their bare skin. Who knew that friction was such a wonderful thing?

Lost in the sensations, he was unprepared when she pushed against his chest, giving herself enough room to maneuver beneath him.

"My turn," she warned, giving his nipple a rough lick.

Michel instinctively planted his hands on the mattress so he could crouch above her, giving her full access.

Chelsea was swift to take advantage, using the tip of her tongue to trace his puma tattoo before she was kissing her way down the rigid muscles of his stomach. It seemed to take an eternity before she at last reached his straining erection. He gasped as she licked the tip, then softly blew across the damp flesh.

Holy…crap.

His fingers dug into the mattress, his head thrown as she took his cock deeper, using her tongue to tease the aching length.

Michel's hips surged forward, his cat purring as she slowly pulled her lips up the quivering length, her fingers reaching to squeeze his heavy testicles.

"Wait." He forced himself to pull out, so close to his climax he could barely breathe. "I want to be buried deep inside you when I come."

Reaching down, he wrapped his arm around her waist and tugged her up the mattress, arranging her beneath him. Then, gazing down, he hesitated as he felt a strange tightness in his chest.

How long had it been since he'd felt such an intense desire for a female?

Never, his cat whispered. Only Chelsea had managed to shatter his fierce barriers to stir his deepest passions.

Slowly lowering his hips, he allowed his cock to settle against the warm dampness between her legs. Her hands lifted, grasping his shoulders as he dipped his head to scatter restless kisses over her face. Then, almost as if she knew instinctively what he needed, she turned her head to the side. It was an invitation Michel couldn't resist.

With a growl, he sank his teeth into the tender curve of neck where it met her shoulder. He felt her shudder as she arched her hips to rub against his hard erection.

There was no need to ask if she was ready.

He could smell her need.

The same need that was twisting his gut into a tight knot.

With gentle care he penetrated her damp channel, waiting for her to wrap her legs around his hips before he plunged deep, savoring the sensation of her hot pussy clenched tight around his cock.

Oh…hell.

She wrapped around him like a glove. So perfect.

Struggling to keep a slow, steady pace, Michel pulled back until the tip of his cock was nearly at her entrance. Then, with a hiss of pleasure, he slammed his way back home.

Chelsea scored her nails down his back, gripping his ass in silent encouragement.

Michel groaned. How had he ever been idiotic enough to try and keep this female at a distance?

Refusing to dwell on how easily he might have denied himself this overwhelming pleasure, he lifted his head to study her beautiful face. Holding her darkened gaze he quickened his thrusts.

Smug contentment surged through him as he watched her cheeks flush, her body tensing before she was quivering beneath the force of her orgasm.

He was the one who'd made her tremble. Who'd held her as she convulsed around his cock.

Briefly wondering how she was going to react when she discovered that he was the only male who was going to be sharing her bed from now on, he shoved aside the worry for later. Right now, all that mattered was the pressure that was swelling to a critical peak.

Wrapping his arms around her slender body, he buried his face in the curve of her throat as he pumped into her at a savage pace. All too swiftly, he was reaching a shattering climax, his body shaking as his cat roared in fierce ecstasy.

***

Locke had a firm rule.

No one was allowed to interrupt him while he enjoyed a traditional English breakfast alone in his office. It was the one time during the day he could eat a meal and read his favorite newspapers in peace.

Unfortunately, over the past several months his peace was more and more difficult to achieve.

And this morning was no exception.

He'd just poured his tea when he heard the sound of running footsteps that echoed down the hallway.

"Now what?" he muttered, folding his paper and rising to his feet as his door was shoved open to reveal one of his more experienced researchers. "Mason, explain to me why my breakfast has been disturbed yet again," he growled, even as he took in the man's disheveled blond hair and the flush on his round cheeks.

Crossing toward Locke's desk, Mason made a belated attempt to smooth his white lab jacket and catch his breath.

"An hour ago two men who claimed to work for Cole Security arrived and demanded to take one of the Pantera females to the Colonel."

Locke hissed, his stomach twisted with disgust. Over the years he'd turned a blind eye to the men who'd used the caged women as their sexual slaves. Either because they wanted to try and impregnate them, or because they were just horny.

This morning, however, he found himself trembling with anger.

"Which one?"

Mason grimaced. “Terri,” he said, referring to one of the most vulnerable of the females.

“I assume you tried to stop them?” he snapped.

“Of course.” The middle-aged man lifted a hand to wipe the sweat from his brow. The past few weeks had been stressful on all of them. “I warned the men that they had to have your approval to transport any of the patients. They seemed to believe the Colonel’s commands overrode any order you’d given.”

Locke’s anger darkened to fury.

This was more than just a man wanting to force himself on a woman. This was a blatant power play designed to undermine Locke’s position as leader.

“I see,” he said between clenched teeth.

“When they refused to listen, I begged them to let me sedate the female,” Mason admitted, his voice shaking.

Locke stared at the man in shock. “They tried to take her without giving her the necessary drugs?”

“Yes.”

“Bloody hell,” he muttered. Why did the idiots think they kept the Pantera in cages? “What happened?”

The researcher shuddered. “Exactly what you would expect. As soon as the female was released she went wild.” He made another effort to wipe his sweaty brow. “And worse, the other patients began to shout out threats. It caused the men to panic.”

God. Damn.

Although Locke hadn’t been there, he could easily imagine the chaos that had erupted the minute the female had been released. The cages were lined with malachite that drained the Pantera of their power, but it didn't entirely incapacitate them.

Which was why they usually kept the patients sedated.

Since the move, however, Locke had dialed back on the drugs, needing their adrenaline levels to return to normal before he could resume taking their blood.

He muttered a curse. "Give me the damage report."

Mason cleared his throat. "They shot the female."

"Dead?"

"Unfortunately."

Locke clenched his hands. It was more than unfortunate. They'd lost over half of the Pantera they'd captured and created during the past three months. And worse, the Pantera now knew they were being hunted. It would be a thousand times more difficult to get their hands on the animals.

Imagining the sheer pleasure of wrapping his fingers around Colonel Cole's thick neck, Locke slowly realized that Mason wasn't finished with the bad-news train.

"There's more?" he demanded.

Mason grimly nodded his head. "One of the Colonel's men backed too close to the cages."

Locke squeezed his eyes shut. Okay. Now it was an official clusterfuck.

"Another corpse?" he forced himself to ask.

"No, but his neck is broken," Mason said. "We sent him to the base hospital, but even if he survives I doubt he'll walk again."

Locke opened his eyes. As much as he wanted to toss the researcher out the door and finish his breakfast in peace, he knew he had to deal with the mess before it spiraled out of control.

"What about the second intruder?"

Mason's expression abruptly hardened. "He fired off several shots that wounded two of our guards before he ran out of the lab." The man's voice revealed his opinion of the intruder. "I assume he was returning to Cole, although there's the hope he'll get lost in the swamp and be eaten by a gator."

Locke allowed a humorless smile to curve his lips. He'd originally shuddered at the thick wetlands that surrounded the edge of the base. He hated the moisture that clung to the air and the scent of rotting vegetation. Not to mention the hideous cloud of insects. But he had to admit it did have a few benefits.

On the point of commanding his guards to go in search of the man, Locke stiffened as his computer made a distinctive ding.

He didn't have to guess who was trying to contact him.

"Clean up this mess and see that the patients are sedated until things settle down," he ordered Mason, waiting until the man had left the office and closed the door before he sat back in his chair and clicked the mouse to open the connection.

Instantly a male with short auburn hair, a thin face, and eyes so pale they looked silver appeared on the monitor.

Christopher Benson Segal. The man who Locke called master.

He'd clearly fed recently on Pantera blood, Locke absently noted, giving the impression he was in his early forties. Locke didn't know his true age, but he suspected it was well over a century.

"Master," he murmured, giving a respectful nod of his head.

As usual, Christopher came straight to the point. "I heard from our Colonel Cole that there was trouble this morning."

Locke leaned forward, not bothering to disguise his annoyance. "He sent two goons into the facility and tried to take one of the females."

Christopher shrugged. "With the money he's paying us, he can take any animal he wants."

"But—"

The older man overrode his protest. "Stanton, you know you're like a son to me."

Was he? Locke had always thought so, but lately he was beginning to wonder if he'd imagined an affection that had been the basis of his loyalty toward this man.

After all, it wasn't as if he'd ever had anyone truly care about him. Not even his drunken mother. So how would he know if Christopher's seeming fondness was genuine or not?

"Yes, master," he murmured.

"Unfortunately, I no longer feel as if I can trust you to work with our newest partners," Christopher continued in smooth tones edged with regret. "Perhaps it would be better if you returned to our headquarters in New York."

Locke sucked in a shocked breath. "All the labs in New York have been closed."

"This will give you to opportunity to clear your head and recall just who rescued you from the gutters of London," Christopher soothed, before offering the final insult. "The Colonel and his men are on their way."

Locke reached to shut off the monitor, feeling…nothing.

It was as if his master's betrayal had stripped him of all emotion. Or perhaps the emotions he'd felt had always been an illusion.

Maybe he'd never stopped being that desperate boy living in the gutters who was willing to sacrifice everything and everyone to survive.

Slowly rising to his feet, he headed out of his office.

CHAPTER 5

Chelsea stared through the windshield of Michel's car, trying to pretend that she wasn't acutely aware of the male seated next to her.

Yeah, like she wasn't going to notice the heat that pounded against her, or the musky scent of Michel's cat that teased at her senses. Or even the brooding gaze that monitored her carefully bland expression.

Or the tension that was thick enough to cut with a knife.

She swallowed a small sigh. When she'd awoken tangled in Michel's arms earlier in the morning she'd instantly gone into panic mode.

It wasn't like her relationship with Locke. That had been easy…convenient. They'd been attracted to one another, and they'd shared an intellectual communication, but there hadn't been any fireworks. Or the sense that she was being consumed by her lover.

But with Michel…

God almighty.

She felt as if she'd been stripped down to her most primitive soul. As if she'd been laid bare for the male who'd given her more pleasure than she'd ever dreamed possible.

It was terrifying.

And oddly exhilarating.

So was it any wonder when he'd tried to discuss the intense night of passion while they lay in bed, she'd instead kissed him until he'd growled in fierce hunger, unable to resist her seduction?

But while he'd allowed her to postpone the inevitable conversation, they both knew it was a temporary reprieve.

Clearly determined to prove her point, he reached out to grasp her chin, tugging her to meet his searching gaze.

"You know, you can't hide from me forever, Chelsea."

Her heart clenched.

He was so gorgeous with his starkly carved features, his stunning green eyes, and his smoldering male sensuality.

Sheer perfection.

No, not perfection, a tiny voice whispered in the back of her mind.

He understood the pain she'd suffered. And he didn't mind her scars.

Another jolt of panic raced through her. "I'm sitting two feet away from you. That's hardly hiding."

His brows drew together, his expression troubled. "Why won't you discuss what happened between us?"

Because I'm terrified you're going to destroy my heart.

"Do you always do a postmortem after sex?" she forced herself to mutter.

He growled deep in his chest, the searing heat in the car becoming suffocating.

"We made love, we didn't have sex. And no, I don't always do a postmortem." He leaned forward, allowing her to see his cat that lurked in the back of his eyes. "But then before last night I'd never been with a female I intend to keep."

He intended to keep her?

"Michel," she breathed, giving a shake of her head.

She hadn't forgotten this male had treated her for weeks as if she had the plague. Or at least that was the excuse she was clinging to.

His lips twisted. "No need for that horrified reaction."

"Just a day ago you considered me the enemy," she reminded him.

His eyes darkened to moss, regret tightening his features.

"I considered my emotions the enemy."

She knew exactly what he was talking about. After the death of her family and her grandmother's subtle rejection, she'd closed off her heart and concentrated on her studies.

Science didn't hurt you.

People did.

"You don't trust me," she reminded him.

"I'm learning." He grabbed her arm as she lifted her hand to bite her nail, tugging it toward his mouth. Sparks of pleasure jolted through her as his lips gently teased her inner wrist. "Just as you're hopefully learning to trust me."

The panic began to recede as she became lost in the warm depths of his eyes.

"What do you want from me?" she breathed.

"To explore the possibilities." He nipped the center of her palm. "Is that too much to ask?"

Exploring possibilities. A tentative smile curved her lips. That sounded…nice. And not nearly as frightening as she'd expected it to.

"No," she said in soft tones. "I think I'd like to explore the possibilities."

"Good." A wicked smile curved his lips as he placed her hand flat against his chest. "And while you're at it, I have a few other things for you to explore."

Her lips twitched. "You wish."

"Every second of every day," he murmured before releasing her hand and glancing toward the building that was bathed in a rosy glow from the morning sunlight. "Let's go."

With the liquid grace that revealed he wasn't entirely human, Michel was out of the car and sprinting toward the side of the fence where he'd left the gate unlocked. Then, pausing long enough for her to catch up, he led her toward the back of the building.

"Are you going to tell me what the plan is?" She kept her voice pitched low enough only a Pantera could hear her words.

He paused at the corner of the building, carefully scanning their surroundings. "I'm assuming Locke has a new facility somewhere on Barksdale."

Once certain they were alone, Michel headed directly toward the van that had been left by Locke's guards.

"So why are we here?" she demanded, grimacing as she tripped over a crack in the pavement.

Unlike Michel, she didn't have the smooth grace of a puma.

She was more in the drunken-sailor category.

"It would take too long to search the entire base, not to mention we risk alerting Locke to the fact we know he's there," he said, surprisingly rounding the van to the back. "The last thing we want is to have him disappear again."

Chelsea frowned, confused about why they were skulking in the parking lot. "I doubt he'll return to this building."

"Which is why I intend to be delivered to his new lab," he murmured, sending her a rare smile as he opened the back of the van and waved her inside.

Her brows lifted. "You want to hide in the van?"

"The driver is supposed to arrive at the lab at exactly eight a.m."

She glanced into the back of the van that was filled with crates that she assumed were empty.

There was no way Michel had left any research files in the hands of his enemy.

"You're sure it's going to Locke?" she demanded.

"We're about to find out."

Without giving her time to protest, he spanned her waist with his hands and hoisted up so she could crawl between the crates. She wiggled between the wooden boxes, her breath catching as Michel crouched beside her, his body angled to make sure no one could get to her without going through him first.

Chelsea shivered, a dangerous sensation piercing her heart.

Just a few days before, he would have been watching her with a suspicious gaze, waiting for her to betray him. Or more likely, he would have had her tied and gagged in the safe house.

Now his first thought was to protect her from the uniformed man who was opening the van door and sliding behind the steering wheel.

Could she offer him the same trust?

The answer came without hesitation.

Yes.

Feeling oddly euphoric, she leaned against his welcoming warmth. She wasn't entirely certain what had just changed deep inside her, but it felt…epic.

In silence they traveled the short distance to Barksdale, coming to a stop as they reached the security checkpoint. There was a low conversation between the driver and one of the guards before they were driving through the gate and down a rough access road to a distant part of the base.

Chelsea grabbed one of the crates as it bounced backward, threatening to squash them. At the same time, Michel was pushing a small gun into her other hand. She sent him a frown before she realized the van was pulling to a halt.

With blinding speed, Michel was lunging forward, knocking out the driver the second he turned off the motor.

Chelsea glanced out the window, catching sight of the distant wetlands before she turned her attention to the rows of small hills that dotted the area around the van.

No, not hills, she silently corrected as a steel door opened in the center of the closest mound and three armed guards stepped out. They were bunkers built by the military to store weapons.

"Stay here," Michel muttered, moving to shove open the back doors of the van.

Instantly Chelsea reached out to grab his arm. "Michel, no," she protested, fear twisting her stomach. "There are too many of them."

A feral smile curved his lips as he gently tugged free of her grasp and leaped out of the van.

Unprepared, the guards took a full second to react to the attack. A second that gave Michel that time to smash his fist into the first guard's face, and kick the second guard hard enough that he crashed into the steel door and crumpled to the ground. The third guard made a valiant effort to fumble for his gun, but in two strides Michel had his hands around his neck, choking him until he joined his friends on the mossy ground.

Taking time to ensure the men were out for the count, Michel returned to lift her out of the van.

"We need to hurry before the guards are missed," he murmured, tugging her past the unconscious humans and into the bunker.

"What's the plan?" she demanded, grabbing the handrail as they jogged down the cement stairs that headed sharply downward.

Her brows lifted in surprise. Clearly the government had defied the marshy swampland by pouring enough cement and steel deep in the earth to prevent any moisture from leaking in.

Another surprise was the unexpected size of the bunker as they stepped out of the stairwell to discover a cavernous central room with several open doors leading in different directions.

"First, we release any prisoners we can find," Michel said, his gaze shimmering gold as he allowed his cat to prowl close to the surface.

"And then?" she pressed.

He shrugged. "Track down Locke and get the hell out."

"Okay." She grimaced, her heart still racing from his earlier battle with the guards. She knew it would be ridiculous to plead with him to be careful, but she couldn't halt the urge to try. "Just…"

"What?"

"Don't do anything stupid."

A mysterious smile curved his lips as he cupped his hand around her nape and gently tugged her forward. Then, lowering his head he pressed a lingering kiss against her mouth before he reluctantly lifted his head and stepped back.

"Do you sense anything?" he asked.

Chelsea gave a shake of her head, as if that could clear her mind.

She was a scientist, not a Pantera spy who was used to sneaking into private labs and battling guards. Let alone indulging in sensual kisses in the middle of danger.

It was all very distracting.

At last closing her eyes, she concentrated on the tiny pulses of energy that marked the presence of life forms in the bunker.

She didn't fully understand how the Pantera blood had changed her, or why she could detect the presence of others, but right now all that mattered was being able to do her part to keep Michel as safe as possible.

"There are seven Pantera and three humans just below us," she at last said.

"That must be where the labs are located," Michel murmured. "Anything closer?"

She pointed toward the doorway across the room. "A human in an office at the end of that hallway."

Heat prickled in the air. "Locke?" he growled.

She gave a lift of her hands. "I can't say."

He hesitated, then leaned down for another brief kiss. "Wait here," he commanded against her lips.

"Michel," she protested as he straightened.

"You're not a warrior. I don't want you hurt," he said, his stark features hard with warning. He wasn't going to negotiate.

"What about you?" she demanded, even as she knew she was wasting her breath. "You're a Diplomat, not a soldier."

A lethal anticipation smoldered in his eyes. "Trust me, I can take care of myself."

Chelsea grimaced as he turned to jog toward the nearest doorway.

Everything seemed to come down to trust.

***

Michel moved with as much speed as he dared down the long hallway. He hated leaving Chelsea alone, but it was too dangerous to lead her through the bunker that was filled with guards.

Or at least, he'd assumed there would be guards.

A growing suspicion slowed his pace as he located the stairs leading to the lower level. Where the hell was everyone?

Surely the three guards who'd met him outside the bunker couldn't be the only security.

At last reaching the lab, Michel peered around the corner, his inner cat roaring at the scent of Pantera blood.

Shit. One of his people had been recently hurt. Perhaps even killed. His jaw locked as fury raced through him. Only his training kept him from bursting into the room and killing any human unlucky enough to cross his path.

Instead, he studied the two men dressed in white lab coats before turning his attention to the cages that lined the white tiled room.

As Chelsea had said, there were seven Pantera being held captive, plus a human female who was cowering in the corner of her cell. But it was the overturned desks and smashed equipment that captured his attention.

There'd been a fight in this room. One that had ended with at least one Pantera being injured.

Bitingly aware that the clock was ticking, Michel entered the lab. He preferred a plan before he tried rescue missions. Too many things could go wrong and an innocent could be hurt. But he could work on the fly when necessary.

Reaching beneath his sweatshirt, he pulled out the second gun he'd tucked in a holster strapped around his chest.

He could easily kill with his hands, but a bullet was quicker when dealing with humans.

He was halfway across the lab when the stirring of the Pantera at last alerted the researchers that they were no longer alone. Turning from the shattered glass they were trying to sweep into a corner, they both dropped their brooms and studied him in resigned horror.

"Not again," the elder of the two muttered.

Again? Michel frowned. He didn't have time for puzzles.

"Get in the cage," he commanded, nodding his head toward one of the empty cages on the far side of the lab.

"Fine," the first man muttered, keeping his hands raised as he backed into the cage along with his nervous companion. Michel swung the door shut, making sure it was locked before he turned toward the cages holding the Pantera. "No, don't," the researcher called out. "You've already got them stirred up. They may look human but beneath the surface they're just…" The man's words trailed away as Michel glared over his shoulder, his eyes glowing with the power of his cat. Both researchers stumbled backward, the younger one tripping over the narrow cot. "Oh shit," the older one muttered.

"Just what?" Michel demanded, baring his teeth. "Animals?"

"Don't kill us," the younger male pleaded, kneeling on the floor. "We were only following orders."

Michel's finger tightened on the trigger. It would be so easy. These men had kidnapped, tortured, and potentially killed Pantera. They deserved to die.

Unfortunately, he knew Raphael would want to question the humans.

"You can plead for mercy once you're in the Wildlands," he snarled.

The older man made a sound of horror. "You can't take us there."

"Okay." Michel aimed the gun at the man's head, enjoying his terror. Yeah, it was petty, but he wanted them to suffer. "Then you die here."

"No." The older man fell to his knees next to his companion, the stench of piss filling the air.

"Christ." Michel grimaced in disgust, dismissing the cowardly scientists as he headed across the tiled floor toward the panel built into the wall. A few seconds later he'd short-circuited the locks that were directly connected to the Pantera cells.

Then, studying the captives as they scrambled out of their prisons, he determined the dominant—a female Hunter with short black hair and amber eyes.

"What's your name?" he demanded.

"Gabriella."

"Are you healthy enough to drive?"

The female shuddered as her body began to strengthen now she was no longer near the bars that were heavily laced with malachite.

"I will be," she promised, her gaze sliding toward the researchers who remained locked in their cell.

Michel knew exactly what she was thinking.

Blood. Death. Dismemberment.

Not necessarily in that order.

He moved to block her view. As much as he appreciated her lust for revenge, he had to keep her focused on the larger picture.

"There's a van parked in front of the bunker," he told her, his voice filled with the authority of his alpha nature. "Get the others out of here."

She nodded before she was abruptly stiffening, her head tilted back as she sniffed the air.

"Wait." She glanced toward the door. "Someone's approaching."

"Shit," he breathed, picking up the unmistakable scent of approaching humans. He knew it'd been too easy to get to the lab. "The guards."

Surprisingly the Hunter shook her head, her slender body vibrating with tension. "No, this is the same smell as the men who arrived earlier and killed Terri."

Michel's brows snapped together. "They're not Locke's?"

"No. They belong to Cole Security, the military contractor. The jackasses sent two men earlier this morning to take Terri. There was a nasty fight that ended up with Terri dead and three humans sent to the hospital," she said, jerking her head toward the broken instruments that had been piled in the corner. "I think there's some sort of power struggle going on."

Michel's breath hissed through his teeth. "I don't suppose we'll be lucky enough for them to kill one another," he muttered.

The Hunter looked grim. "Doubtful."

Michel turned to the Pantera huddled together in the center of the lab, drawing comfort in being near one another.

"I need those capable of fighting to stay with me," he said. "And one volunteer to lead the others out of here."

With speed that would astonish a human, three Pantera had moved to stand next to the Hunter while a Healer entered the cell to scoop the terrified human female into his arms and then herd the other two Pantera out the door that led to an escape tunnel.

Michel followed behind them, closing and locking the door before returning to the Hunters who'd spread out as they prepared to fight.

"They're coming," he murmured, lifting his gun even as the female Hunter gave a low laugh of anticipation.

"Bring it on," she rasped, holding up her hands to reveal four-inch claws.

Michel blinked in shock, his gaze lifting to take in her long fangs and the pure gold of her eyes. *God. Damn.* It should have been impossible outside the Wildlands. "You can shift."

She shrugged. "Only partially."

"How?"

Her lips twisted in a bitter smile. "Whatever shit they were pumping into me, altering my DNA." She slashed her claws through the air. "Now I get to use my new powers to kill them."

He dipped in head in respect to her fierce spirit. "Ironic."

"Justice," she said, turning toward the six humans who entered the lab.

Justice. Yes. Michel returned her smile as they charged forward, easily overwhelming the intruders.

CHAPTER 6

Chelsea heard the sound of approaching footsteps only a few minutes after Michel disappeared.

Instinctively she tried to follow him, only to realize that she wasn't going to have time to cross the central room before the intruders entered. With no choice, she darted down one of the long hallways, entered the first office she could find and locked the door.

She breathed a sigh of relief only to give a small squeak of alarm as a hidden door behind her slid open to reveal the male she'd once called her lover.

Hastily she hid the gun behind her back, her gaze taking in the lean face that was pale and almost gaunt in the flickering fluorescent light. He looked as if he'd aged ten years in the few weeks since she'd last seen him.

"I thought that was you on the security camera," he murmured, crossing the small room to stand directly in front of her. "Hello, Chelsea."

A bittersweet pain sliced through her heart. She would always care for this man. No matter what he'd done. But she wasn't a fool. If he realized why she was there he wasn't going to let her walk away.

Not again.

"Locke." She twisted her lips into a faux smile. "I was looking for you."

He arched a brow. "Were you?"

"Yes, I—"

Her words were cut short as he pressed a finger to her lips. "Please, don't," he murmured, his voice surprisingly rough. He usually took great care to maintain his polished accent. "The one thing we always had between us was honesty. Don't ruin that."

She grimaced. He was right. They'd never been able to lie to one another.

"Okay. I came with a Pantera," she said, allowing her hand to fall to the side so he could see the gun she was holding. "They needed me to help track you."

He barely glanced at the weapon, a sad expression softening his too-thin face. "I assumed it would come to this."

She blinked, hating the sight of him looking so defeated. "Then why did you release me?"

"Because I love you."

"Not as much as your master," she reminded him, knowing that this man would never truly understand love.

"I swore an oath." He shrugged. "What sort of man would I be to turn my back on my pledge?"

"He was never worthy of your loyalty, Locke," she said.

"Probably not."

She narrowed her gaze in surprise. Over the years Locke had never flinched, no matter what outrageous sacrifices Christopher had demanded. Now she sensed that Locke was no longer as blindly devoted as he'd once been.

"He's betrayed you, hasn't he?" she said, her sympathy genuine.

He grimaced, reaching toward her. "It doesn't matter. All I care about right now is getting you out of here."

Chelsea stepped back, avoiding his grasp. "I'm not leaving without Michel."

"Michel?" Locke frowned, then abruptly dropped his hand. "Oh. You mean the Pantera."

She met his gaze squarely. She wasn't ashamed of her growing connection to Michel. Hell, a part of her wanted to shout it from the rooftops.

"Yes."

Pain darkened his eyes before he was giving a shake of his head.

"You can't stay, Chelsea," he insisted. "It's not safe."

She stiffened, recalling the sound of footsteps that had driven her into this office. "Is this a trap?"

"It's not me you have to worry about, Chelsea," he assured her. "Not ever."

Her mouth went dry. Something was going on. Something bad.

"Tell me what happened."

He hesitated, a flush of shame staining his cheeks. "Christopher has sold our research to a military contractor," he at last admitted.

Chelsea had already suspected the truth, but still, his confession came as a punch to the gut.

"You promised—"

"It's too late," he interrupted.

"He's right. It is too late," a male voice floated across the room.

Chelsea jerked her attention toward the open door that Locke had so recently used to enter the room. *Gah.* Why had she let herself be distracted by her former lover? She didn't think he'd deliberately set her up. His expression was as horrified as her own. But still…

She studied the large, bald male dressed in a uniform who was pointing a gun directly at her heart.

"Slide the gun over here," the man ordered.

Locke moved to stand at her side. "Do it, Chelsea," he warned in soft tones.

Bending down, Chelsea placed the gun on the floor and slid it toward the man.

He watched the weapon skid to a halt at his feet before he turned his attention to Locke.

"It's unfortunate that it's come to this, Locke," he said, his insincerity patently obvious.

"It's unfortunate that your men killed a helpless female," Locke countered, not bothering to disguise his own disdain.

"I'm sure it was an accident." The man shrugged. "Now, you have something I want."

"Here." Digging into the front pocket of his pants, Locke pulled out a key card and tossed it toward the intruder.

The man muttered a curse, his round face hard with anger. "I want your computer, Locke."

Chelsea glanced at the man at her side. Had he hidden his computer to keep the military from getting their hands on his research?

"I haven't had time to bring it from my other office," Locke said.

"Now, Locke," the intruder snarled, deliberately glancing toward Chelsea. "Unless you want another helpless woman to die today."

Chelsea's heart slammed against her chest, her fear thundering through her.

Where was Michel? Was he safe? Had he escaped with the other Pantera? God, she hoped so.

"Wait," Locke snapped, stepping forward.

The man tensed, his patience clearly at an end. "Your computer," he repeated. "I won't ask again."

Locked nodded and Chelsea reached to grasp his arm.

She wasn't a hero. But there was no way she could live with herself if she knew she was responsible for the military using her research to create genetically altered mutants.

"Don't, Locke," she pleaded.

The stranger gave a small wave of his gun. "I will shoot."

Chelsea glared at his pudgy face. Shit. She really, really disliked the bastard.

Locke held up one hand while he shoved the other in the pocket of his suit jacket.

"Just relax," he muttered, pulling out a small disk drive. "I have all my research on this."

A sickening anticipation smoldered in the man's pale eyes. "Hand it over," he commanded, his gun swinging in Locke's direction. "Slowly."

Locke stepped forward, only to halt and glance over his shoulder with a wistful smile. "I really did love you, Chelsea."

"Locke?" she breathed, already knowing what he was about to do before he dropped the disk drive on the floor and crushed it with his heel. Then, with grim determination, he charged forward. "No," she screeched, watching in horror as the stranger squeezed the trigger and pumped three shots into Locke's chest.

Her every instinct urged her to rush to Locke's side as he tumbled to the ground, but she fiercely forced herself to turn away. He'd sacrificed himself so she could escape. She wasn't going to dishonor him by doing something stupid.

Even as she turned, however, the door was being smashed open and Michel rushed in with a female Pantera.

His swift glance took in Chelsea, making sure she wasn't hurt, before he turned to absorb the sight of Locke lying face-first on the floor and the large man who was now pointing the gun in his direction.

Astonishingly, the female with short, dark hair gave a low, chilling laugh.

"This one's mine," she growled, leaping across the floor even as Michel was rushing forward.

Shots rang out, and Chelsea pressed a hand to her mouth, terrified one of the Pantera might be hit.

But with a blinding speed, both managed to avoid getting hit, and, grabbing the man by the arms, Michel held him captive as the female lifted her hand and slashed her nails across his throat.

No. Chelsea blinked in shock. *Not nails, but claws.*

Four-inch claws that ripped through the man's beefy neck as if it was butter.

Blood flowed and chunks of flesh hung from the man's throat before Michel was tossing him aside like he was a piece of trash.

A part of Chelsea was horrified. She'd just watched two men die.

No matter what they'd done, it was an awful thing.

But a larger part was so relieved that Michel was alive and unhurt that she barely noticed the bodies sprawled on the floor as she launched herself straight into his waiting arms.

***

Michel stood at the edge of the clearing, taking pleasure in the sight of the Pantera who'd gathered to enjoy a collective meal among the wooden tables spread across the sun-drenched glade.

It didn't matter that there was a crisp edge to the afternoon breeze, or that there was still danger lurking beyond the edges of the bayou. For this moment they were celebrating the newest members of their pack.

It'd been three days since their return to the Wildlands from Bossier City. So far they'd managed to get the Pantera they'd discovered settled in new homes. The human female was still in the medical clinic being treated for shock.

He'd intended to devote his time since their return to mating with Chelsea and disappearing into his home to enjoy a few months of complete privacy.

Unfortunately, he'd had to meet with Raphael and Parish to reveal what he'd discovered in the military lab, as well as the death of Stanton Locke and Colonel Cole. It'd taken precious time. And on top of it, Chelsea had been busy examining the Pantera who'd been locked in the cells. She hoped she could discover exactly what had been done to them and if it might be a danger to them.

They'd barely had a minute alone.

The only thing that'd saved his sanity was the fact that he'd demanded she at least agree to become his mate before they'd ever left Bossier City. There was no way his cat could have maintained any patience without the promise that he soon could claim his mate.

Now he impatiently waited for Chelsea to finish speaking with Gabriella who was trying to adjust to the fundamental changes made to her, as well as her seething anger toward her kidnappers.

He'd hoped to escape with his female before he could be caught. Unfortunately, he was still waiting when Raphael appeared at his side, his golden gaze skimming over the crowd as they began to break away and return to their jobs.

There was an unmistakable satisfaction in his expression.

Despite the fact they hadn't yet located Christopher, and the Goddess knew how many other enemies lurked in the shadows, they had managed to rescue several of their people. And best of all, Stanton Locke was dead.

The bastard had even given his life to protect Chelsea.

A win/win as far as Michel was concerned.

Waiting until Raphael had reached his side, Michel nodded toward the graceful Colonial-style building that stood on the far side of the clearing.

"Has Xavier managed to salvage anything from the disk drive?"

"Not yet, but you know the Geeks." Raphael smiled with wry amusement. "They're not going to give up until they manage to investigate each fragment."

Michel snorted. "Better them than me."

"No shit." Raphael rolled his eyes. "It's tedious enough to sort through the piles of files you managed to rescue from the lab. I would have had much more fun with Parish, torturing Locke's guards for information."

"Have you discovered anything of value?" Michel demanded.

Raphael grimaced. "Nothing that leads us directly to Christopher. But I did manage to find…" The older male's words trailed away as Michel watched Chelsea finish her conversation and walk in his direction. She was wearing a tight emerald sweater and even tighter jeans that made him growl with excitement. Oh hell. He was going to have pleasure ripping those off her as soon as he got her alone. Suddenly he felt Raphael lay a hand on his shoulder. "Michel, are you listening?"

His rapt gaze never wavered from Chelsea's beautiful face framed by satin curls that shimmered like flames in the sunlight.

"Nope." He shook off his friend's hand. "This meeting is going to have to wait until later."

Raphael made a sound of impatience. "But it's important."

"Not as important as my mate," he assured his friend.

"You've mated?"

"Not yet." A jolt of anticipation raced through Michel as he headed toward the female who'd taught him that his emotions weren't something to fear, but to be embraced. "That's something I intend to take care of right now."

"But we need Chelsea," Raphael called from behind him. "There was a female who was brought in who's suffering. She's obviously been experimented on by Locke and she's—"

Michel gave a dismissive wave of his hand. "Later. Much, much later," he muttered. His heart leaped with a pure joy as Chelsea flashed her rare, perfect smile as he reached her. Then, knowing the time was at last right, he leaned down to sweep her off her feet, cradling her tight against his chest. Damn. She felt perfect in his arms. "Hello, beautiful."

"Michel." A lovely flush stained her cheeks as several nearby Pantera clapped in gleeful pleasure at his open display of possession. "Have you lost your mind?"

He leaned down to press his lips to her forehead. "I think we already established that I lost it the moment I caught sight of you," he reminded her.

She chuckled as he carried her away from the glade and toward his home that was tucked in a lovely tangle of cypress trees.

"Sometimes you're a very, very good Diplomat," she assured him.

His cat brushed beneath his skin, his claws already slicing through his skin in preparation of marking her.

"I intend to be an even better mate," he swore.

She shivered, her ready desire scenting the air with sweet arousal. "Mate."

His gaze swept over her face. "Are you ready?"

Wrapping her arms around his neck, she regarded him with all the love he'd tried to deny.

"Michel, I've waited my entire life for you."

STRIKER

LAURA WRIGHT

CHAPTER 1

Twelve

I am a nerve. Raw and humming. The one inside me, pushing, pushing, calling me by my name—my number—keeps me intact. It keeps me from breaking apart and existing no more. It came to me…how long ago? Hours. Days? I don't remember what those are. Did I ever know?

Pain. Burning. Hungry pain.

It has pulled out of me.

I growl at it. *More. More.*

It knows what I mean. It understands my sounds. It understands my teeth. I'll bite it. Consume it, if it doesn't come…

Ahhhhh…

It's flipped me. Something soft catches me, my face, my belly. My hips are yanked up. It's inside me again. Deep. And it's thrusting. I feel…better. But not enough. I need the wash of its semen. Spreading over me. Inside me.

Healing me.

Eyes wet. Mine. Why? Pain…but not in my body. My heart. Will this end? Ever end? Not who I used to be. My name is not Twelve. And yet it is.

Hands cup my breasts. I press into them. They are good. Big. Hot. Squeezing me. It—the one inside me—gives me what I want. Always gives. It is good.

My claws dig into the softness. Claws. That's what they are, yes? I think.

What is thinking?

It makes sound when it's inside me. I like this sound. My blood is rushing. My insides are exploding. I follow it.

I am coming. It is coming. My body grips, holds tight, sucks until I get want I want. The wash. It hits hard. So hot I can't breathe. And then it spreads…the relief…inside and over and throughout.

I lie there, panting. Content. My tears dry.

My eyes are clear. I look and see. Where I am. The room. Pretty. White and blue and cool, and warm. I've been here before, I think.

What is thinking?

Then I'm covered. My skin is very warm. Like my insides. And I am safe.

It makes me safe.

I sleep.

***

Striker

Seventy-two hours of constant fucking makes a male hungry. The Pantera female is sleeping. I stand at the door watching her, downing a sandwich. I hope she gives me at least fifteen minutes this time. I need fuel. I should change the sheets. Lot of come on that white cotton. Not to mention the rips and tears. For some serious debauchery, they've given us one sweet-ass cabin. It's like Martha Stewart decorated it, then said, "Let's dial this shit back a little, friends."

She stirs, and so does my cock. I'm ready. Hell, I'm always ready. It's part of the reason they chose me. The other part I refuse to acknowledge.

My eyes run over her. Long, pale, naked limbs, small breasts, an ass that will no doubt consume my thoughts for years, long, thick black hair that falls near to the top of that ass—and an angel face that displays every emotion imaginable even though her mind is not her own. She's lying on her belly, still asleep, her ass pink from my ready hand. I 'met' her just seventy-two hours ago, but I know every inch of her.

Every. Inch.

A Pantera male—a normal, sane, feeling Pantera male—would have claimed this female as his own by now. Couldn't help it. Not only does she give off an unusual and debilitating scent that would have every male in the Wildlands fighting to fuck her, but something happens to our kind with long-term rutting. We connect. We bond. That's why I was brought in. I'm not your normal, sane or feeling Pantera.

I don't connect with anything.

She stirs again, but this time she rolls onto her back and shows me that sweet, glistening pussy. My cock fills with blood. I haven't even bothered to put on underwear. What's the point? I finish off the roast beef, down the bottle of water on the bedside table, and get back to business.

This female needs sex. Semen. Constantly. And I'm here to give it to her. Until she returns to sanity.

If she returns.

Her eyes open then and she finds me looming over her. Her eyes are almost otherworldly—the palest blue I've ever seen—and they light up when they scale down my chest and abdomen and hit my cock. As usual, she growls. The sound is savage, like she wants to tear me apart and consume. But instead of getting the hell off the bed and out of the cabin, I inch closer. Because every time she does it—that low, feral growl—my dick weeps.

I grab her knees and instantly she lets them fall to the sides. Her eyes pinned to my dick, she slides her hands down her flat belly to her pussy and opens the wet lips for me. My cock releases a drop of come. It's the only thing on me that feels deeply.

She growls again and snaps her teeth. If I don't get my tongue on her or my cock inside her, she'll bite me. She's already done it twice. Granted, I barely felt it because I was coming, but it broke the skin. Was going to call in one of the female docs, but both gashes stopped bleeding pretty quick, and there wasn't time for a sew-up job anyway. Besides, she doesn't seem to like others around. Watching. Can't blame her, with what she's been through.

I crawl between her legs. She's deliciously slick, and I'm always hungry for pussy. Shit. Seventy-two hours in bed. While there's a war brewing outside this cabin. Things a Hunter should be a part of. Military using the blood of our kind for…what? Research? To create some kind of super soldier? And Stanton Locke's 'master' is still out there, doing damage, spending billions to keep himself alive. And then there's the secret enclave of

Pantera in the Florida Everglades that Hiss has gone to.

I should be working.

Not *playing*.

But Raphael and his new second-in-command, Shadow, think this female might have valuable information to share. I just need to get her to a place of coherence so we can unlock what she knows.

Again she growls at me, her teeth bared.

I grin and whisper softly, “Easy, Twelve. You will have what you need.”

The moment I drop my head, her fingers are threaded in my hair, and her nails dig into my scalp. I’ll be bleeding before this is over.

My lips close over her clit and I suck.

CHAPTER 2

Twelve

There are memories locked inside my mind. I know I have a mind. And a body. And a heart. A cat. And a hunger for this…*it*. This *thing*—no. This creature? No…

My eyes open. I stare. Hard. Try to focus, to see what is truly there. The thing…creature…its eyes—darkest green—slam into mine. The eyes make my insides feel hot and soft. Not like the others. Why? Why is the creature different? My vision cuts left. Over the hard planes of the creature. Light. From the window. Windows. I love windows. They give me hope. I used to live outside the windows. Right now the light is gray and peaceful. But the air is cold. I feel it rush over my skin. I need more warmth, heat, come from the creature—NO! STOP! It is not a creature. *Think. Think.*

Male.

The word is long and strange as it's dragged from my brain. A shudder goes through me. Males scare me. Yet, I want them. Need them to survive. They want me too. All the time. It didn't used to be this way…I think. I think…I can't escape it. But this male—is different. Not like the others. No madness. Only hunger. Only desire. And touching. Heat. He is holding me. He is inside me.

I open my mouth, try to speak. But nothing comes. I want to know the creat—the *male's* name. If he has a name. The others…just numbers, like me. No looking into my eyes. No words. No holding. I was food. Something to consume.

"Are you going to bite me again, my little puma?" the male asks as he continues to thrust inside me.

I like his voice. I try. Push for words. My throat. But nothing comes. Can I speak? Can I do anything but growl and grunt and groan?

His eyes flash, not with anger over my struggle, but with understanding. He leans down and covers my mouth, takes my tongue inside and sucks. The feeling is wondrous, and I moan as my body turns to fire. It wasn't like this. Before. With the others. As humans watched. Staring, assessing, while they put pencil to paper.

I'm so filled. He fills me. My sex and my mouth and everything in between. The creature—NO! *Think.* The male. This male. Who is he?

Where am I?

In that moment, he drags his mouth away and his eyes are on mine again. I'm going to break.

Open. I wrap my legs around him and let him pound into me. Let him fill me.

Fuck! Goddess, if only I could have you, he rasps.

Hot, wet, he comes inside me. And as I follow him, as I cry into the cold air and the gray light, something clicks in my mind. I reach for the male and clasp his face. "Your name," I whisper. "Who are you?"

His eyes, once glazed, so green, focus on mine. "Fuck, you're back?"

Where was I?

And then, like a tsunami, my mind is deluged with images. Of the clinic. Of the drugs, and the needles, and the pain. Of being taken…from where? My home, my family…then male after male. They want me, and yet they don't. So much pain from desire. But nothing works. Not my hand. Nothing except the males…

Then days of silence. No males. No nothing. All pain.

And blackness.

Fear. It's inside me. I think I'm screaming.

Pain. In my arm. And the warmth is gone. The safety. I'm not filled anymore. Not held anymore. The green eyes…

"What the hell happened?" I hear a female voice. So worried, but far away.

"She spoke." The male. The creature. I need him. Want him. "But then…shit, it was like it was too much for her. She went crazy. Started screaming."

I'm fading. I reach for him. But it's cold air.

"You can get dressed and go," the female says. "I'll take it from here."

"You're sure?"

"Go."

I can't stay awake.

I miss him already.

***

Striker

"You look fresh as a fucking daisy," Pride says the second we shift out of our cats and enter the Suits' headquarters.

I don't answer the young Hunter. He's new and therefore unclear about the way I work. Quiet. Capable. Done. Instead, I take the stairs two at a time.

"So," he presses, following close behind me. "How was it? Your…" I can practically hear him grinning. "Assignment?"

"Over." The mansion is running at high speed today. Suits and a few Geeks, all focused, deep in conversation or eyes glued to their screens. Only a handful look up as we walk by, and just one acknowledges my presence. Life inside the Wildlands has changed now that the outside world is aware of our existence. I constantly feel on guard. It's a shame, but it's reality.

"Come on, brother," Pride continues, irritating me as we walk down the hall. "Give me something."

“I’m not your brother.”

But he isn’t listening. Which doesn’t bode well for him. “Three days with a gorgeous female puma who’s so amped up all she wants is to get fu—”

I have him against the wall before he can say another word. No. Before he can say *that* word. My puma is scratching to get out, but I harness it. It would kill this male if I let it.

“Listen to me,” I say softly. Behind me is a conference room. It’s gone quiet. “Say another word about her, and I’ll see that you don’t say another word ever again.”

The blond male’s blue eyes widen. “Shit, sorry, all right? Just talking. Getting to know one another. That kind of thing.”

I release him and back off. “Not interested, Rookie.”

“Lian and Rage were right about you,” he says, glancing around at the Suits watching our interaction. “I should’ve listened.”

“Yes, you should’ve.” I turn and head for Raphael’s office. My quick anger surprises me. Especially in regard to the female. Normally, I would’ve ignored the stupid male’s comments altogether.

The leader of the Diplomats is seated behind his oak desk, long blond hair pulled back in a leather thong, nose in a bunch of paperwork. Without looking up, he points to the leather chairs facing him. “Have a seat.”

Pride practically vaults into the chair. "What's up, boss?" he asks as if nothing at all just happened outside the door.

Raph looks up, glances at me. I shrug. *Young cub.* What else is there to say? He nods, then begins, "As you both are aware, there is a group of our kind in the Everglades."

"The Cadejo," I say.

He nods. "Hiss is there now with his mate, Gia, and her family. I have not been in contact with them. We thought this might happen, but I don't like it. I think it's time to connect. I want to establish diplomatic relations with them. That's where you come in."

"Cool," Pride says, grinning.

"Is it just going to be the two of us?" I ask through gritted teeth.

Raphael's gold eyes find mine. I'm hoping to see sympathy or humor there. But it's all seriousness. "Shadow will be going too. I don't want to send too many Pantera, or all Hunters. I don't want them thinking we're infiltrating. Plus I need my most experienced here in the Wildlands."

I nod. "Understood."

"We want to make friends with the Cadejo, Striker," he says pointedly. "We may need them some day." *Soon*, he doesn't say. But he doesn't have to. I know exactly what's at stake with humans sniffing around our borders and men like Locke imprisoning and using our kind.

Leaning forward in his chair, like a child waiting to see his first Dyesse lily bloom, Pride asks, “When do we leave?”

“Three days.”

“Hot damn. I’ll be ready.”

I stare at Raphael. The male is a master at keeping every thought, every feeling hidden. But so am I, and I know there’s something he’s not telling me. Something he’s waiting to tell me.

And I know I’m right when he turns to my young partner. “Pride, go to Shadow’s office. She’s waiting for you.”

“What?” he balks.

“Yes,” I say quickly. “Tell your sister hello for me. Tell her I have great sympathy for her.”

The young Hunter growls low in his chest, but gets up and heads for the door. He may be a young, rookie cub, but he is Pantera, and would never defy Raphael.

As soon as he’s gone, I look at the leader of the Suits. The seriousness in his eyes is gone. In fact, he’s trying hard to suppress a smile.

“That wasn’t very nice.”

I sniff. “Neither was putting me with an infant. Especially when you know I have the nurturing skills of a mother wolf spider.”

“You will not eat this young. He’s entirely too big.”

“Don’t be so sure. I almost took a bite out of his larynx just outside your door.”

“He does ask inane questions at times.”

“Or disgusting, insulting, degrading ones.”

Raph's brows draw together. "What do you mean?"

I shake my head. "Nothing." But he remains silent, waiting—it's his way—so I halfheartedly explain. "He wanted details about my…mission with Twelve."

"Ahhhh…" He eyes me, studies me for a moment, then leans back in his chair. "She's doing well."

"I didn't ask."

He nods. "You didn't, but I thought maybe you'd like to know." He inhales sharply, curses. "She's telling Doc Julia about what happened to her in there. What Locke and the others did to her. All in the name of baby production and more pure Pantera blood for his master. I can't believe our own were treated this way." His puma flashes, the shape in his eyes changing. "I want to kill every last one of them."

We will. It'll take time, but we'll have our revenge. "Did she offer any details about who else held her captive? Who worked beside Locke? Names? Locations?"

His eyes move over my face, like he's trying to understand my lack of ferocity over what was done to Twelve. *Being a prisoner takes many forms, boss.*

"Not yet," he says. "There's much to ease out of her."

I cock my head.

"It will take a gentle hand."

"There's a reason why you sent Rookie to visit his sister, isn't there? Not to just shoot the shit with me?"

He nods. "She doesn't want to stay at the clinic. And after what she's been through, I completely understand why."

What this has to do with me… "So let her stay elsewhere."

"We have. We…will. But—"

There it is. The *but*. The reason I'm sitting here.

"She isn't comfortable staying alone."

The emphasis on that last word has my gut tightening. It was just three days ago that Raphael called me in here for Mission One: fuck the female back to health and sanity. Now he's looking for what? Someone to guard her?

My eyes flash ferocity at my superior. "No."

He sighs. "It's just until you leave for the Everglades."

"No."

"Goddess, Striker," he grinds out. "There isn't that option. Not if I order you to."

I push forward in my chair, aware of the aggression of my body language. "Raphael, think about this—"

"I have."

"No, you haven't. Not if you keep coming up with the same answer. You know me. What I'm capable of, and what I'm not. And there's a lot more things in the 'not' department when it comes to females. How you can believe I'm the best Pantera for this—"

He cuts me off. "I don't."

The tone, and the truth, stall me. "Then…why?"

He shakes his head. "It's not me who wants you for this job, Striker. I do know you."

My brows go up.

"It's her."

"What?" I exclaim.

He looks as mystified as I feel. "She feels safe with you."

I laugh. The idea is so fucking preposterous…I mean, sure I can keep her safe in the physical sense. No one would get to her, unless they stopped my heart. But she's so not safe in the feelings and emotions department. I stopped knowing how to talk to, comfort or support females a long time ago. Somewhere around the time my mate left me for my twin brother.

I push out of my chair.

"Where are you going?" Raphael demands.

"To speak with her. Reason with her. Where is she?"

He doesn't say anything.

"Raphael?"

"You hurt her more than she already is, and I swear I will kick your ass myself."

"That's my fucking point," I tell him. "That's what I'm trying *not* to do."

He looks away. "Fine. I told you. She's back at the cottage."

Right. I head out the door. The cottage. Martha Stewart Hell. I sniff, shake my head. The poor female. No doubt she's confusing my three-day fuck mission for true care and concern. Time to show her the real Striker. The one no female wants by her side. On top of her or between her legs, yes. But by her side, never.

CHAPTER 3

Twelve

It's hard to believe I'm safe. It's hard to sit here on this couch, in this lovely cottage, with the sun streaming in through the window, and not shake. Not anticipate someone jumping out from another room or behind the door and sticking a needle into my skin—then just a few seconds later, a hungry, vacant, drugged-up male climbing on top of me…

"What else can I get you?"

My heart kicks in my chest.

But I have to believe it. I have to keep reminding myself that I am not a victim. Not anymore. Because it's the only way I'm going to stay lucid—and find out the truth.

I glance up. The woman, the human doctor, Julia, is coming out of the bedroom. Her long blond hair is pulled back in a ponytail which sort of swishes as she walks. She's helped me, at the clinic and with coming back here. She's been nothing but kind. But do I trust her? Absolutely not. I trust no one. Especially medical staff.

Especially doctors.

It was a doctor who took me, abducted me from my home, and brought me to one of the labs. Sold me.

If I could only remember where that was…where home is… It's at the very edges of my mind.

"I'm fine," I tell her, forcing a smile. "Thank you again for the clothes."

"It's my pleasure. And incredibly easy as we're the same size." She smiles brightly, and I get the distinct impression she wants to chat, make friends. But I'm not interested. Everyone who's come into my life since the abduction, even those who've acted kind and concerned, have hurt me or betrayed me. There's only one who's ever truly made me feel safe.

The screen door bursts open and a male wearing blue jeans and a faded gray T-shirt walks in. He's pissed, ferocious, and when he spots me on the couch, his eyes run over my body. A slow tingle makes its way up my spine. My body remembers him, even though my mind does not. This tall, heavily muscled Pantera, with short hair the color of night and eyes so dark green—and so fierce, I imagine everyone who stands before him trembles.

Everyone beneath him, too.

"Okay," he says, stalking over to me, completely ignoring Dr. Julia. "We need to talk."

My heart stirs with pleasure at his voice, and I instantly feel a calming sensation move over me. *Yes*, my body says, *this is the one*. Unfortunately the doctor's body is on high alert. She immediately gets in between us and puts her finger in the male's broad chest.

"Striker," she begins, her tone a blatant warning. "You need to go back outside and come in again with a new attitude."

"No, he doesn't," I say quickly, before he can respond.

Striker turns to me, Julia too, and I give the woman a nod. *It's good. It's fine.* Surprised, she shakes her head, but gets out of the way. Green eyes blaze down on me. Curious. Irritated. It's strange, but I don't remember what this male and I did in this house over the past three days. I mean, I know because I was told, and because I have my sanity again. But I don't remember it. All I have is a feeling. A deep connection. A sensation of well-being.

With this male, I am whole and protected.

I glance at Julia. It's time for her to go. "Thank you, doctor," I say pointedly.

She takes the hint, but is clearly concerned and hovers for a moment. "I can stay for awhile."

"It's okay," I tell her.

"Parish is working, and I don't have to rush back to the clinic."

This time, Striker shoots her a severe glare. "She wants to be alone with me, Doc. Take a hint, and a hike."

"With how you're behaving," she says, "do you think that's a good idea?"

"It doesn't matter what he thinks," I say, rising from the couch. I have endless amounts of weakness inside me. My brain is sharp only when I get sufficient sex, my heart is mutilated, my nerves are shot…but I'm out of that hellhole. I'm alive, and I'm going to take what I want. What I deserve.

And what I deserve is to put the pieces of my life back together.

"I'll call if I need anything, Dr. Julia." I walk to the door and hold it open for her.

She looks from Striker to me, then back at Striker. She releases a breath. "You'd better behave yourself," she warns before grabbing her bag.

He sniffs. "Sure thing."

"You have my cell number," she tells me as she heads out into the late afternoon sunshine.

"I do. Thanks, Julia."

I close the door and return to the couch. As soon as I sit, I pat the leather cushion beside me. "I'm glad you came, Striker."

He remains standing. "It wasn't my choice, Female."

I pretend not to feel a slight jab of pain. He doesn't want to be here. No. He doesn't want to be *ordered* to be here. I understand that. "Regardless, I appreciate it."

"Maybe you can tell me why."

"I need your help."

"With what?"

"I want to go home."

It wasn't the answer he was expecting, and he takes a moment to process it. "And where is that exactly?"

I sort of do this half laugh. Shrug. "I don't know. Can you please sit down?"

With a frustrated grunt, he drops into the seat beside me. He's so big, long and formidable, and yet I know he would never hurt me. Not in a physical way.

"I'm hoping you can help me find out where I belong," I say, my eyes connecting with his. "Help me remember."

His dark brows knit together. "And how would I do that?" His voice is so deep, with a hint of a growl.

I lift my chin. "Same way you helped my mind return."

His jaw goes instantly tight, and he grinds out, "That's over. That was a dire situation. One I was called in to fix."

I flinch, the little stab of pain in my belly flaring again. It's bizarre. This male is so dark, so cold, so curt. The way he talks, I'm nothing more than a mission to be completed, and yet my feelings toward him, whatever memory my cells have captured, is completely the opposite.

"It's been promised that you'll stay here," I say. "With me, for the next few days."

"To guard you," he clarifies. "Protect you."

"Not have sex with me?" I have no pride. Not when it comes to finding out the truth about my past.

"No." He turns away from me and eyes the other side of the cottage. "I need a shower. Then we'll discuss dinner."

My shoulders droop a little as he walks away. All I want is to remember who I was before I was taken. I have to know that female again to be able to leave this female behind. Striker is the key to unlocking my memories. I know it. But I truly despise the fact that after all I've been through, all the males who have come sniffing so over-eagerly around me for years, I have to work to attract this one. This one who seems unaffected by both the pheromones those cold bastards at the lab put into me, and the time we spent together over the past three days.

But I will see to it. And I won't be ashamed. Seducing Striker will be new ground for me. And in the end, it will be worth it.

***

Striker

She can't cook. I, on the other hand, kick ass in the culinary department. About thirty minutes ago, a bunch of groceries were delivered to the cabin door. No note. And no Pantera in sight. Like Twelve and I are fucking newly mated or something.

I venture a quick glance in her direction.

Wearing a pale pink terrycloth robe, she stands against the counter and watches me as I stir the sauce for the chicken parm. It's unnerving. How she looks at me.

Here's the thing: it's not that I'm unaffected by whatever shit those bastards put into her. Pheromones, love potions, voodoo charms… Or her natural hotness. I am. I just don't allow desire to rule my mind and actions. Even if it's crushing desire.

Shit, especially crushing desire.

Problem is, I've had this female. I've ruled her body for three days straight. I know what she feels like, tastes like. Her cream is still on my tongue, for fuck's sake—and I want more.

At just the thought, my insides flood with heat as my cock remembers her too.

"You can go chill out somewhere while I finish this up," I suggest, my voice thick with annoyance. At myself, this time. Not her. My thoughts are running rogue. It's bullshit. But I know if I'm continually around her, I might fuck her again. And if I fuck her again, I'll lose some of the control I've harnessed for the past seven years.

And I can't let that happen. I nearly drowned before.

"No, thanks," she says. "I like watching you."

I turn and growl at her. "That wasn't a suggestion."

Her eyes flicker with tension, but she doesn't jump or move or run. As I'd hoped. Instead, she talks.

"I know you're angry with me."

Fuck. I turn back to the sauce. "I'm not angry. I'm not anything."

"Well, I know you don't want to be here."

"It's pointless. My job was completed. I don't like repetition. It breeds…confusion and attachment."

"Oh for shit's sake," she grinds out. "I'm not asking for a mating, Striker. So if that's what you're freaked out about, don't be. As soon as I find out who I really am and where I'm from, I'm out of here. There's no confusion. No attachment. I just want sex."

My cock twitches. I put down the spoon and sigh. At least I intend it to be a sigh. I think it comes out more like a growl. I cut her a look. Her thick dark hair's piled on top of her head. I remember how it looks in every light. Those pale blue eyes too. And her skin…

"Is it that you don't find me attractive?" she asks.

I bark out a laugh. "Yeah, that's it. You repulse me, Twelve."

"Well then, is it you?" Her eyebrows lift in a very mocking way. "Things not working down there when you want them to?"

I flash her my puma.

Her lips twitch. "Then I see no problem. I don't want anything from you but this." She grabs the two strips of terrycloth at her waist and unties them.

"Don't—" I grind out.

But she's not listening to me. She shimmies out of the robe, lets it drop in a pool at her feet and stands there, her hip against the counter, naked.

Every inch of my body erupts. Can't help it. Can't stop it. My skin, my cock, my tongue, my hands—they all know her. And to know Twelve is to want her. She has the kind of face and body painters dream of capturing. Expressive eyes, full lips, pale skin, dangerous curves, perfect vee of curls between her legs, and breasts so round and high, a male's hands can't help but pulse with anticipation.

I turn back to face the stove once again and start dishing up the chicken parm. When I have two full plates in my shaking hands, I stalk past her—beautiful perfect, naked her—and head for the porch.

For air.

Cold, night air.

"Bring the wine on the counter," I call back. "And a couple of glasses."

Maybe drunk Striker will have better luck at keeping his hunger for this female under control.

CHAPTER 4

Twelve

It's a little cold to be sitting outside naked, but I make it work. Across the table, Striker shovels food into his mouth without looking up. He hasn't met my gaze in nearly five minutes.

"I know you want to know too," I say.

"What?"

"Where I'm from. How I got into the lab. How a Pantera female was made into a breeding machine." I laugh. A thankful, yet bitter sound. "A breeding machine who never bred."

His eyes lift at that. He has the most beautiful eyes. Terrifying eyes. Soulful eyes.

"That's right," I say. "With all the drugs and the males and the endless… They never got what they wanted."

His face pales, and his nostrils flare with ire. "Fuck, Twelve, thank the Goddess."

I nod. "Agreed."

"I'm sorry if that was too flippant or insensitive."

"It's fine. And true." I'm not looking for pity. I'm really not. I'm talking to him, being real with him, because I want him to understand the depth of my need. How coming out of something like that, a prison for both my body and my mind, makes me desperate for freedom and answers and truth.

To the point where I'll sit at a table, on a porch, without clothes—the sunset bathing my naked skin in orange light. My eyes move over the view, the intense green, the massive cypress and the bayou rushing softly by.

"Has the Wildlands always been your home?" I ask him.

He nods. "Haven't ventured outside of it all that much. Have a trip coming up, but mostly it's just hitting up The Cougar's Den."

I look back at him. "What is that? A safe house?"

A slow smile spreads across his face. A smile is rare for him. I've never seen it—that I can recall—but it looks amazing on him. I wonder what it would feel like to have that smile above me as he moves inside—

"It's a bar," he says, cutting off my thoughts. And good thing too, I suppose. "In La Pierre. A town not far from our borders."

"Do a lot of the Pantera go there?"

He nods.

I'm suddenly alive with excitement. "Can I go there?"

He shakes his head.

"Oh, come on. Why not?"

"Look at you."

I do. For a second, I glance down at what I already know. I'm naked. Then find his gaze once again. "I can always put some clothes on. Doc Julia gave me a couple of really nice things."

"Good," he says, dropping his napkin on his plate. "Why don't you go do that, then? Like, now."

"So that means we're going to this Cougar's Den?"

"No."

I scoff. "Then forget the clothes."

He sighs. "You know we can't go out, Twelve."

"Because I'm hideous."

"Exactly."

I laugh. "Because I smell."

That smile returns, and this time it hits those emerald eyes full blast. *Gorgeous.* I think I need to fan myself.

"You most definitely smell," he continues. His chin drops and he says almost covertly, "Too fucking good for it to be safe. I'll be knocking males out right and left."

I'd like to see that, I almost say.

"And that wouldn't be fair to them, now would it?" he adds.

Party pooper. I fiddle with the rest of my chicken. "Would I be a total bitch if I said I don't care about fairness? Or those males? I just want to do something normal. Something every other Pantera gets to do."

He studies me for a moment.

"I mean, what's the point of being free, if you're really not?"

He inhales sharply, and a shadow crosses his gaze. "How long has it been since you shifted?"

Just the question sends my heart into my gut. It's a question I stopped asking and thinking years ago. I shake my head, and sudden tears threaten to close my throat. "I can barely recall it. Early on in the lab, I was given so many drugs, first to bring my puma to the surface, then to repress it. This happened to many of us. Even the males who…you know…"

His jaw tightens. "I know."

"They wanted to see our cats, use them, test them, but soon they realized, even without a full, magical shift, how powerful we were."

His lip curls. "Scared you would rip them apart if given the chance?"

"Hell, yes," I respond passionately. "Because I would have."

Green eyes tear into mine. Probing. I'm naked as I sit here, totally vulnerable, and yet his gaze doesn't flicker downward even once.

"Finished?" he asks.

"With dinner?"

He nods.

"I am. And thank you, it was really good."

One black eyebrow lifts. "How about dessert?"

Just the way he says it makes my skin tingle, and my nipples tighten. If only he would notice. If only he would take advantage of it. I want my memories returned, yes, but truly if I don't have sex again in the next few days, I'll lose even more. Maybe this. I won't let the madness claim me again. I'll go to another male if I have to.

I try and keep it light. Keep the banter. The flirtation. "Did the Pantera Delivery Service bring something sweet?"

"I haven't looked."

Oh. My heart kicks inside my chest. Was the worry for naught? Is he going to give me what I want? "Then what do you suggest for dessert?" I ask.

"A run."

No. Not what I want. My brows slam together. "I'm confused. You want to go jogging?"

"No." He can't contain his grin. "Our pumas. Out there. Exploring the Wildlands."

This time, my heart kicks for a different reason. A longing I haven't felt—or maybe haven't allowed myself to feel—in a long time. "I really don't know if I can."

He pushes his chair back and stands up. "You can. And quickly. Before we have a visitor, or a Hunter on patrol." His nostrils flare. "If a male is even close to this cottage, he'll come searching. And if he finds you, I may have to kill him."

"Oh, come on."

"I'm dead serious, Twelve."

His eyes confirm that statement. Flashing all kinds of possessiveness. This male doesn't make sense.

"Wouldn't you be relieved, Striker?" I challenge, standing up. "Someone to take the job you don't want?"

His face hardens, and his whole body goes rigid. "You don't understand. Don't get—" He cuts himself off, shakes his head.

"What?" I press. I feel naked now. "What don't I understand?"

"Nothing. Just forget it. I want to go for a run. A hunt. And I want you to come with me." His eyes shimmy down my body, and a low, soft growl rumbles in his chest. "Try, Twelve. Close your eyes and go inside."

"I don't feel her at all," I say, but close my eyes anyway. I want to know my cat again. At least, I think I do. I'm so out of touch with who I am, what I am… "How can I bring her out if I don't feel her?"

I hear him move closer to me. Feel the heat off his body. "She's just been locked away," he says softly. "Like you."

A shiver runs through me and I open my eyes. He's a couple feet away, his expression intense, entranced. And behind his eyes, I can see the fearsome cat reflected.

"She wants to come out," he tells me. "I promise. Close your eyes."

I do, and I try again. I breathe deeply and call upon her. Is that how I did it before? I doubt it. I listen for her. Wait to feel her. Feel something. But…it's white noise. Nothing. Tears threaten and I bite my lip.

"Don't you dare," he growls.

My eyes stay closed. "What?"

"Give up."

I'm not about to. It's just frustrating. But I won't. I go silent again, and push down…deep…I call for her. I don't know her name, but I call for her…

"Maybe this will help," I hear him say.

I crack one eye, and by the time my vision focuses, Striker is in his puma form. He's glorious. A massive black cat with emeralds for eyes. He glares up at me, growls and hisses. And when he does, I feel something stir…inside. Of me. Something that wishes to growl back.

I close my eyes again. And again I push down. As I do, I feel Striker's puma brush against my left leg. I inhale. Soft, yet hard muscle. Again, I feel the stirring inside. Both in my heart, and in my sex. I gasp as I feel him on my right, his massive head nuzzling my hip. *There.* She's there. *No. Here.* I start to tremble. This is right. I go inside and she springs forth. I feel the rough tongue of Striker's puma on my right ass cheek just seconds before I dissolve into my cat.

A roar collects in my ears. My puma's ears. And my eyes open. His cat is facing me, looking me over. And I feel…

Goddess, I *feel.*

He snarls at me, then turns, bounds down the stairs and takes off into the coming night.

I don't need any more invitation than that. I spring from the porch, hit the rough ground and follow him.

***

Striker

My cat wants her cat.

As we run along the bank of the bayou, as we dart in and out of the cypress and weeping willows, and now, as we sit side by side, on the healthy, magical border of the Wildlands, The Cougar's Den in the distance, my cat wants her cat.

I am different inside my puma than most. Acutely aware of who I am without this fur and muscle and fangs. Of the male I am. I can think totally separately. Reason. And yet with Twelve beside me, I find I am unable to control my puma. In fact, I am pretty sure it wishes to control me.

I glance her way. She's a stunning cat. The color of rich mahogany wood. Her eyes are a deeper, darker shade of blue, rimmed with black. She stares at The Den in the distance, and the town beyond. What is she thinking? Does she want to run? Leave the Wildlands, and start fresh on her own?

I wouldn't blame her, but the thought fills me and my puma with a shocking sense of dread. Not because I would fail in my mission to get further information about this female and her history and her time in the lab. For Raphael, and for the cause.

But because I can't stand the idea of her out there, unprotected.

I am her protector.

A soft growl rumbles in my throat, causing her to turn and look at me. Those dark blue cat eyes narrow and she rises and inches toward me, stopping only when her nose is nearly touching mine.

My cat wants her cat.

Christ, I've never even thought about taking a female in puma form. I know some do. Especially mates. But it's never crossed my mind.

Until now.

And then she leans in and licks me.

Her tongue, pink and rough, across my face. And my cat goes rigid. Inside and out, humming with a need it's never experienced before. The ultimate hunt.

She sits back on her haunches and waits. Her eyes wide and curious. A question. *Will you take me this way, Male?*

I'm up on my feet in seconds, and start circling her, growling, mewling, showing her my teeth. Showing her what could very well be sinking into the back of her neck if my cat goes rogue. Around I stalk, rubbing myself against her. Making sure she has my scent on her fur. It is absolutely certain that I would kill any male who so much as looked at her right now.

The thought fills me with sickness. And dread. That would be the ultimate possession. *Mine. Mine. Mine.* A low snarl erupts from my throat. If my cat takes her cat, we will be bound. The puma is not like the male. It cares nothing for history and pain, complications and vows. It never reacted to the one who left me, the mate. She was never the puma's choice. Only mine. The beast is smarter than the male, clearly.

No. You don't get to have her. It's my male self speaking now. *You don't get to have her if I don't.*

Madness wants to claim me. I can't allow it. I shut my eyes and I force my shift. Painful as it is, because the cat wants so desperately to remain. To climb on her back. To bite her neck.

To take her, hard and unyielding.

But I push and push and push until I feel *it* recede and *me* come forward. Feel my clothes coat, then cover, my skin. Feel the breath enter through my mouth, not my nose.

Twelve's puma is watching me. She looks resigned. Gone is the playful cat who was purring as I rubbed against her. I hate to see it, but it's necessary.

Then before my eyes, she shifts too. From mahogany cat to beautiful naked female. She doesn't move, doesn't even try to cover herself. She is incredibly comfortable in her nakedness. I, on the other hand, wish I had a fucking blanket to throw over her. What if a Hunter comes by on patrol? He would see her perfect pale flesh, her round bottom, those pink nipples that are tightening into points as we sit here.

She's shaking her head at me. "You deny even my cat?" she says. "I told you, I don't want anything serious or lasting or permanent from you."

Even though I'm in male form, the puma hovers just below the surface, and my voice is low and feral. "My cat would."

She gives me a confused look. I forget she has no memory of the time when she was a puma, when she was around pumas. She has no idea of our ways, rituals or mating.

"It's not just the cat," I continue with a bitter edge. "A connection like that might make me, the male, end up wanting something from you. Something I shouldn't want." My voice lowers. "Can't want."

Twelve is silent for a moment as she seems to consider this. Around us, the sounds of night on the bayou intensify. And the light from the moon overhead seems to spotlight the six inches of ground between us.

"Who?" she says, finally.

I stare at her, confused. "What are you talking about?"

"Who did this? Who caused this?" She reaches out and touches my temple.

Her fingers are soft and cool and I have to restrain myself from leaning into them or turning my head and licking them.

"Who fucked with your brain?" she continues, her eyes pinned to mine. From the cat's dark blue to such pale intensity. "And you can tell me because if anyone understands all of that, it's me."

I refuse her. Myself, too. "Don't know what you're talking about." I want to pull away. Shit, I want to run away. But I can't.

"I won't push you for answers," she says. "In fact, I won't ask again. I just want you to know that pain is pain, no matter how it comes into our lives and rearranges and takes over and destroys. It's all the same. And if you want to tell me, I would listen without judgment. I would listen."

Inside my chest, something heavy resides. It's not a heart because that was taken and crushed long ago. Maybe it's my lungs. After all, I do feel slightly breathless.

Her fingers sweep over my cheekbone in the most soothing way. I love it and hate it equally. But I want it to stop. How I accomplish that, however, is idiotic. I lean in and kiss her neck. One kiss. Right where her pulse thrums against the skin. I hear her breath catch and, as I thought, she drops her hand.

This is it. I should pull away completely now, shift back into the puma and take off toward the Wildlands. But the scent of her skin has invaded my nostrils and my bloodstream. My dick is growing harder by the second, and I don't know if it's the drugs in her system or the pheromones, but I've never wanted to taste anything more.

My tongue laps at the band of muscle, then I scrape my teeth gently across it. She hisses and arousal scents the air. She must've been turned on before. Inside her cat. Or maybe it was the cat. Regardless, she is wet and hot now, and I want to bite her. Mark her and taste her blood. I groan against her skin, but resist. Instead, I continue kissing my way up her neck to her ear. With a snarl of need, I lick the shell. She releases a breath and leans into me. Shivers. And another waft of intense desire hits my nose.

Goddess, how does one resist?

My teeth attack the lobe and nip. She cries out and arches her back. My eyes flicker open and I see that her lips are parted. She's breathing heavy. For one second, I swear she's going to shift into her puma. I feel…something…against my tongue, or inside myself. But the second passes, and I'm suddenly being shoved to my back.

I hit grass, and without a word, Twelve is on me, straddling me, her pussy grinding against my zipper. My brain fries and I grab her backside and thrust her forward, until she's sitting on my chest. Gorgeous pink pussy surrounded by dark, wet curls.

The perfect view.

She gives me a hiss of annoyance. Wants me to stop staring. I oblige, but give her something else to hiss about. I slide two fingers deep inside her. She gasps and I growl. She's so tight and hot, and all I want to do is replace my fingers with my dick. As I slowly pump inside her, I watch. Eyes closed, mouth open, she rocks. Her body is magic; pale, supple flesh writhing under the light of the moon. My thumb brushes over her clit and when she lifts herself a few inches off my chest, I snarl. Her pussy is glistening, the brown curls a temptation to my hungry mouth. I remember how she tastes, how my tongue went searching for the hot, swollen prize inside.

She's riding me now, my fingers drenched in her cream. Up and down, impaling the two digits like she should be impaling my cock. My brain is full of that image. Well, that and how her perfect breasts are bouncing, the nipples hard and tight and high, as she moves.

"Stretch over me, Twelve," I command. "I need your sweet tits in my mouth. I need to suck them as your pussy is sucking my fingers."

"Oh, Goddess," she groans, but instantly complies. And in seconds I've latched on to her left nipple. Moaning at the sensation, she freezes in place, and lets me work her over, nipping and sucking at her hot little tit while I thrust up deep inside her.

"Look at me," I command as I press the pads of my fingers against the sensitive part of her pussy. The part that makes her cream.

The part that makes her come.

I remember. Fuck, I don't think I'll ever forget.

And she does. All over my fingers and down her right thigh. Her eyes clinging to mine. And this time, she knows who I am. Not the 'it.' Not the creature.

"Striker," she breathes.

"Oh, yeah, beautiful," I grind out, pumping her gently as she starts to come down from her climax. "You feel so fucking good."

"That was…" she breathes. "Goddess, that was amazing. But…"

Our eyes meet again, and a flash of ire moves through me. Why? Fuck me. Why? I don't want to hear the *but*. Because I know what it is. What she wants. And my cock is screaming for me to give it to her. It's all I can do not to unzip, lift her up and drop her down on the thing. Hell, it's already straining against my fly like a goddamned monument, wanting to get out.

But she says it anyway.

"It's not enough."

Gut tight, everything tight, I ease my fingers from her and pull away, come to my feet. While my back is turned, so she can't see me, I slide both digits in my mouth and just taste. I stifle a groan because she's so fucking sweet. And because I hate how I've allowed my brother and my ex-female to steal the pleasure and desire I want to feel in this moment—that I want to take.

"Time to go home," I say, though as soon as the word is out of my mouth I want to steal it back. That cottage is no home. It's a temporary hiding place. For us both.

As I turn back to face her, Twelve is already shifting into her cat. But I don't miss the look in her eyes. Those pale blue orbs are hazy with climax, but it's there. The ugliness. The frustration. The regret. And it bites at my insides.

She wastes no time in doing exactly as I've suggested. Leaving me, dashing across the marshland, heading for the cottage. And this time, it's me who follows her.

CHAPTER 5

Twelve

Sleeping in a bed—an actual bed, after years of a hard, antiseptic-smelling pallet on the floor of a cell in the lab—is pure heaven. Sleeping alone? Not so much.

I don't understand this about myself. I should be content, more than content, with a huge, comfortable bed all to myself, with no fear of being watched or wakened or snuck-up on. But I'm distracted. And…

I can still feel his fingers inside me.

His mouth is imprinted on my neck.

I fall back against the pillows. *You need to stop. Get your mind off him. I promise you, his mind is off you.*

In the other bedroom. Door closed.

I reach for the iPad the Pantera Diplomats have given me, and turn it on. I'm pretty unfamiliar with technology. Especially the newer gadgets. I saw workers at the lab using them, but we weren't allowed close enough to see how things worked or what was available on the different devices. Along with the clothes, Dr. Julia gave me a tutorial on the basic working of the small computer, and a recommendation as to what to watch. A television program called "Scandal," that she swore was "The greatest thing ever."

I blink at the screen and scan the contents, check out the different programs, and decide to just go with the woman's advice. Political drama, sexy, suspenseful. Sounds good. I push Play and tuck in for the first episode. Halfway through, I'm wishing I had popcorn. Halfway through the next one, I'm totally hooked. And halfway through the third, there's a knock at my door.

I stab the Pause button and glance at the clock. Eleven fifteen. What is he doing?

"Striker," I call.

The door opens, and he walks in wearing only a pair of gray pajama bottoms. Really unfair. They hang low on his hips, and make my mouth water.

I clear my throat. "Is it too loud?"

"What?"

"My show." I point to the iPad.

His brows draw together. "Oh. No."

I wait. Both for him to give me a reason why he's in here, and for him to put on a shirt. Seriously, it's like being a diabetic and having a hot fudge sundae shoved in my face. The male has *the* most perfect body. A trim waist that vees upward to broad shoulders and powerful biceps. Then there're the waves of corded muscle and the line of hair leading down to his…

"I want to apologize," he says finally.

It takes my brain a second to register what he's saying as I've been temporarily held captive by his beauty.

"For what?" I ask.

He looks around, uncomfortable. "I don't know."

"Come on, Striker."

"Okay. Treating you like—"

"A mission?" I finish for him. Then because I've been watching hours of relentless flirtation, I add, "Or refusing to keep treating me like a mission?" I can't help myself. My mouth quirks up at both corners. The thing is, I'm not angry with him, or insulted. I understand that he wants zero attachment. I understand that it's a life raft he seems to cling to. But I can't make that my business. I have enough to think about with my own sanity and future. "Listen, it's fine," I tell him. "No harm done. Promise."

Unconvinced, he comes over and sits on the bed, near my hip. "I feel like I have to explain."

"You really don't."

"I do."

I heave out a breath. *Perfect.* I was just getting over him. Well, thinking about him, anyway, as I watched this crazy show. And now he has to sit in front of me without a shirt, showing off his hip bones and his green eyes and those hands and fingers…

My sex clenches in memory as those eyes hit mine full force. They're dark, and I don't mean in hue. They're tortured. I know that look well. I saw it every day, on many a face, for many years.

"This isn't something I talk about," he says. "Shit, it's not something I think about. I pretty much act like it doesn't exist. I believe that's worked fairly well. But then…you were given to me—" He stops, shakes his head. "I don't mean it like that…"

"I know," I say. *But why do I wish you did?*

He leans in. "Listen, I was mated, Twelve. Up until about seven years ago."

My heart stutters. Not at all what I was expecting. "What happened?"

"She decided she wanted to be mated to someone else."

The set of his jaw, the way his eyes refuse to connect with mine. My breath holds fast in my throat, because I feel this is the crux of everything with him. The very reason why he doesn't want to bond with me or anyone. This is the head-fucker I was trying to get him to tell me about at the border.

"Who was it?" I ask. "The Pantera she…went to. Did you know him?"

"Very well." He laughs softly. Such a bitter sound. "My twin brother, Lynx."

My mouth drops open. Oh Goddesss…

"We were close. He was it. All the family I had. Until her."

"Was?" I say, my breath stalled. Was the male *dead*? Had Striker been so angry—

"No, no. He's very much alive, Twelve. The female too. They're both Suits. They live here in the Wildlands, but are constantly traveling. I haven't seen them in about a year." He sniffs. "It's been a decent year."

"I'm so sorry," I say. "I can't imagine that kind of betrayal."

His eyes pin me. "Can't you?"

A soft, sad smile touches my mouth. "It's something different when blood, when family, is involved. He crossed a line that is hard to come back from."

Striker nods. "It tore me apart for a long time. But I survived it. The pain, the betrayal, all of it. And you will too."

My eyes move over his handsome face, and those melancholy eyes. Yes. I will survive it. But not like this. Like him. Closed and untrusting, his fear of being hurt again driving every decision he makes. Especially the ones regarding his heart. As I sit on my big bed, the iPad on my lap, the moon full and bright outside my window, I'm grateful to my soul or my heart or whatever brought me through that hell and didn't leave me completely jaded. I want happiness. I want love. I deserve it so much. Striker does too. I hope someday he can see that.

"I wanted you to know this so you understand where I'm coming from," he says. "*What* I'm coming from. I can't mate again. Even if the urge is there." He releases a breath, shakes his head. "I don't want you to think I'm not hungry for you, Twelve. You're the most beautiful female I've ever seen. You make my insides liquefy. And the shit on the outside go marble-hard." His eyes run down my body. What he can see of it, anyway. "I'd love to pull back these covers right now and take you again. Get back inside you again. But, fuck me, Female, sex leads to feelings of mating. Not just for the female, but the male as well. This male, anyway. It's how I'm built."

My skin is vibrating at his words. In the lab, I needed sex. I needed a male's semen to make me clear and whole and momentarily comfortable. But as I sit here, what I need—what I *want*—is sex for reasons that have nothing to do with survival, or memories retrieved. I want this male inside me to bond.

Just like he said.

I swallow the saliva that's pooled in my mouth. "I understand."

"Twelve—"

"No," I say. "I really do." I force my eyes up, make myself look at him. Show him my strength. "I know that wasn't easy for you. I'm glad you told me."

He doesn't say anything. He looks miserable. I wish I could help. But he's made his choice. "Goodnight, Striker."

He looks stunned for a second, then pulls it back. "Sure," he says in a forced voice. "Night."

I watch as he stands up and heads for the door, the muscles in his back making the muscles between my legs clench. I force my attention back to the iPad. With a tap, my show resumes, and I'm overwhelmingly grateful for the sound, the distraction.

"That 'Scandal'?"

His voice. Again. A little lighter now. I look up. He only made it halfway across the room before turning around to face me again. I laugh. "How'd you know?"

A wicked grin spreads across his features. His first real smile since we got back to the cottage. It spreads through my chest and pings my heart. "Parish and Doc Julia are obsessed with that fucking show. They've got everyone watching it." He snorts. "The president's a dick."

I immediately race to defend Fitz. "Well, Olivia's not doing all that much to resist him, now is she?"

He gives a casual and incredibly sexy shrug. "I suppose I guess when you're… What do the books say? Hardcore into each other? Made for each other?"

Is that what the books say? "I don't know about all that. I'm only on the third episode, so this could be just a short-lived affair."

"Doubtful." He pauses and just sort of stares at me.

I sorta stare back.

"That's where I stopped," he says. "On the third episode. I had work. Lot of shit going on right now. I can't believe Parish is on the second season with what's happening outside our borders. Inside too, for that matter."

He's killing me. I can tell he wants to stay, but won't allow himself to ask. What do I do? I mean, of course I want him here, next to me, hanging out. Hanging in. But he just came in here to tell me he can't do things that bind himself to me—or any female.

And yet, I very easily say, "You can watch it with me, if you want."

His eyes flicker with heat.

"On top of the covers," I clarify. "And these clothes"—I point at my pajamas, which consist of a dark blue tank and fuzzy blue and white pajama bottoms—"will stay on, I promise."

He laughs and heads back over to me. When he lies down, stretches out on the king bed, I'm surprised by how much room he takes. He has such a long, big body. Like a tree you want to climb.

But of course, I don't.

I turn back to the iPad.

"What part are you at?" he asks me.

"I'm only five minutes in," I lie. "So why don't I start from the top?"

"You're too fucking good to me, Twelve."

My heart flickers with tension and heat, but I don't say anything to that. Not when I hit Play. Not when the opening photography clicks erupt. And not when Striker leans in and rests his chin on my shoulder.

***

Striker

Three hours of watching TV in bed and I'm hungry. Not for food, mind you. Or for Olivia Pope—who incidentally is the object of many a Pantera's wet dreams lately. *Thank you, Parish and Doc Julia.* No, my hunger is for the female beside me. It's been like torture. The sweetest torture. Sitting here, hearing her laugh when shit gets funny, gasp when shit gets scary, then going very quiet as the Prez takes Olivia again on something solid, somewhere secret.

That last bit is where the true pain lies. Her silent yearning. The scent of her arousal pushing into my nostrils. Female likes to watch. Oh, the things I could show her if I wasn't such a closed-off pus—

"Sorry," she says, glancing over at me. "I can't help it. It's pretty potent normally, but this is probably making you crazy. Feel free to go."

My voice has an edge to it when I scold her. "Female, you have nothing to be sorry for. Ever."

"It doesn't bother you?"

"Course it bothers me. I want to fuck the shit out of you right now."

She gasps.

I laugh at her stunned expression. "But when don't I want to fuck the shit out of you?"

I expect her to laugh too—hell, I'm trying to keep things light—but she doesn't. Her expression is a little strangled. As if she's not sure how to feel.

"You know, this is almost over," she says. "We can pick up tomorrow."

"Not a chance," I say. Then, desperate to bring back the mood of the past three hours, I growl at her playfully. "I have to see what's going to happen. I'm fucking hooked on this shit now."

Her mouth twitches and her eyes sparkle.

And my dick goes hard.

"Why don't I hold this for awhile," I suggest, taking the iPad from her and placing it right on top of my growing tent. "You know, I have to say, it pisses me off…"

"What?"

"Well, Liv is great and all. She's smoking hot, for sure—"

"Okay, okay," Twelve cuts me off with a quick yet good-natured glare.

"Not as hot as you, of course."

"Point, Striker."

"He's married."

She goes quiet, her eyes probing mine.

I shrug. "Yeah, I know it's fiction."

"That's not why I'm staring at you."

"Why are you?"

"What's her name?"

My brows come together.

Her expression softens. Her voice too. "The female who left you? Your mate?"

I inhale sharply. Oh, shit…I wasn't expecting… Twelve is constantly surprising. "Farrah," I tell her.

"Well, she's an asshole."

My eyes widen. And when I replay what she has just said, my lips twitch.

"And a fool." Her chin tilts up. "I kinda want to kick her ass."

Oh, fuck, and I kinda want to kiss your lips. For hours. No one has ever championed me before. Not even after Farrah left. Or maybe they did, tried to, and I didn't let them. Maybe this female is just different. Special.

She's turned away, looking at the computer in my lap again. She reaches over to push Play.

"What do you think, Striker?" she says, pointing at the President's wife on the screen. "Team Mellie?"

I grin. "Absolutely."

But when she drops her head on *my* shoulder this time, I can't help but think I'm Team Twelve. All the way.

CHAPTER 6

Twelve

I wake up in the worst-best way possible. In Striker's arms. He's lying on his back in the middle of the king, sunlight streaming in from the windows to the right, making his skin glow. And just as I'd imagined it last night, I'm practically scaling him like a tree. I'm flush against his hard, hot side, one leg draped across his groin, one arm stretched over his chest.

And I'm wet.

Hot and tight and wet.

He's supposed to be in his own bed. I mean, I'm trying to respect his boundaries, desires. But they're really screwing with my own.

I move, just a little, slide my leg down a couple of inches so I can see the rock-hard sex that's been pressing against my inner thigh.

My breasts tingle against the blue cotton of my tank as I spy the head of Striker's impressive cock peeking out from the confines of his pajama bottoms. He's pink and stretched, and I can't help myself. I reach for him and brush my thumb over the smooth head. Instantly, I feel it twitch, pulse. And as I watch, a drop of semen leaks from the small slit. I lick my lips. At this incredible organ that feels so familiar to me. I know it's been inside me…but have I—my lips curve upward—tasted it?

Again, I brush my thumb over the head. Silk over marble. But this time, Striker groans in his sleep and presses himself into my hand. My core clenches. And tucked inside the lips of my pussy, my clit swells. My heart is beating so fast with desire that my mind is starting to shut down. Not only do I want to go down on this male, wrap my lips around him and go to town, but I think my sanity is starting to slip. Nothing huge or significant yet. But it's there. Ready and waiting.

Not yet.

It's not until that moment that I realize I've eased down the waistband of his pajama bottoms and have his cock in my hand. I fist him and release a breath. My fingers can barely contain him. I stroke him once, twice, just to see how he reacts. And when he groans, growls softly and once again drives his hips up and pumps himself in my hand, I start making my way down his body.

Inches of tan, taut skin meet my gaze, but the only stop I make is his left hipbone. I'm captivated by it. I kiss it, lap at it, then on a soft growl of my own, I bite it.

A sharp intake of breath meets my ears. I give his hip one last kiss, then drop my head and take his cock into my mouth. My insides melt. Goddess, he's perfection. Soft, hard and tastes so fine.

"Twelve," Striker rasps.

I glance up, release him only to the tip, and say against the wet, pulsing head, "Do you want me to stop?"

His green eyes are open and hotter than I've ever seen them. He glares at me and snarls, "Fuck no. I want you to take me deeper."

I smile, then suck him in. All the way to the back of my throat. He groans and jacks his hips up gently, trying not to hurt me, I'm sure. But it might just be a pain I would enjoy. Gripping him possessively, I guide him in and out, then swirl my tongue over the head and inside the slit.

He curses, groans. "Faster, beautiful," he growls. "And grip my cock tight. Fist me while your mouth fucks me."

His words fuel the already out-of-control fire inside me. Squeezing him, I bob my head, taking him deep and out again in quick, wet movements. As my pussy clenches, I feel him expand. Then pulse. He curses again and grabs the back of my head. He's coming. And though I want to taste him, drink him down, I wish this incredible cock was inside my sex right now.

"Shit," he grinds out, stiffening as I continue to suck him off.

And then he's coming. Hot and delicious down my throat. I've never known such hunger. I swallow and swallow, and stroke him. I've never felt so powerful. So sexy.

So desperate for a male to take me.

And for a brief second, I think he's going to. The moment I ease my mouth away, he's up and reaching for me, his eyes the color of the bayou at night. It's the closest I've seen this male look like his cat. It's hot, and a little scary. And I brace myself for impact.

But then it's over. His attention diverted, his shift taking place even as he's leaping off the bed. I track him as he rushes to the window, goes paws up. He's heard something. He scans the landscape, growls.

"What's wrong?" I ask.

In seconds, he's pushing away from the window and shifting back to his male form. Tall, broad, tan, still half erect and irritated. "We have company."

My heart lurches. "Not males." I would've sensed that.

"No. Females. And too damn many of them." He stares at me on the bed. I'm clothed this time. He's not. His jaw tightens. "Stay where you are. I'll take care of them."

***

Twelve

Striker's 'taking care of them' was basically demanding to know what they wanted, telling them they couldn't have it, and storming back into the cottage and getting on his cell with the leader of the Pantera.

Not that it did any good. The four females, including Dr. Julia, are determined to engage with me. They brought a picnic breakfast, and an attitude that Striker could take a hike, or a run, or a shower, and leave the ladies to it. And I have to say, I appreciate their tenacity, even if my mind, and maybe my heart, are back in bed with the sexy Hunter.

"More, Twelve?" Genevieve Burel asks me, holding up a lovely platter of scrambled eggs with cheese sprinkled on the top. The blond female is definitely the most interested in my well-being. Which I guess makes sense since she's a Suit. According to the leader himself, the Diplomats are determined to find, recover and protect all rats.

"I'm fine, thanks," I reply with a genuine smile. "They were delicious."

"We have another new cook," she says, setting the platter down on the massive blanket. "He studied in New Orleans. Makes everything a little spicier than usual, but delicious."

"I think I love spicy," I say. "If my very full stomach is an indication. I may need a food-coma nap later."

Genevieve laughs.

"You'll tell us if you really do get tired, though, right? Or just want to head back inside...?" Ashe Pascal trails off. The mate of Raphael, the leader of the Pantera, gives me a gentle, understanding smile before turning to check on her sweet baby who's fast asleep in her carrier.

"Of course," I say, sipping some juice. "But I think I'm good. I love being outside."

"Nothing like sunshine and fresh bayou air," Keira puts in, tossing another bit of bacon into her mouth. The gold-eyed Hunter is beautiful and strong and mated to another Hunter called Bayon. "Can't imagine you had much outside time in the labs."

She's also blunt.

And I like it.

I prefer it to tiptoeing around the subject, or pretending I've been away on some vacation—where my memory was strangely stolen from me, and I smell like sex walking to any male within spitting distance.

But Ashe isn't cool with the Hunter's frankness, and she shoots her a very exasperated look. "She doesn't have to talk about that, Keira."

Dr. Julia nods, a cup of coffee in her hand. "We didn't come here to pry."

Keira gives me a sheepish smile. "Sorry."

"It's okay," I say. "Really. The truth is we were never let out. Never had fresh air or sunshine. It was like prison. And most of the time, I was all by myself in my cell, or cage, whatever you want to call it. It was hard. Lonely."

"That's what he said, too," Keira tells me. "The first word he used…" There are a couple of throat-clearings, and her voice trails off. She looks at the other women, confused.

Both Genevieve and Ashe shake their heads and sigh.

"Who are you talking about?" I ask.

Cheeks pink, the Hunter picks up a silver bowl and offers it to me. "More strawberries?"

I catch her eye. "Keira."

Genevieve is quick to say, "Don't."

But I'm not listening. "Please," I press the female.

"I'm not going to lie to her, you guys." She faces me again, her expression taut. "One of the males from the lab. One of the males who was used…like you…with you… He's here."

Around me, the females get quiet. I let this information sink in, allow my mind to roll back. It's funny, strange, that I can remember everything from my time in the lab and nothing about what came before it. "Is it Three?" I ask them.

Keira's eyes bug. "How did you know that?"

My heart squeezes at the confirmation. I can't believe he's here. "Unlike many of us, he remembered his life before the lab. He had a mate. She was his best friend, and he talked about her all the time. Even when—" I break off for a moment, then say, "The loneliness was killing him. He was a good male, and I'm so glad he'll be reunited with—" The look on Keira's face stops me. "What?"

"This was supposed to be a relaxing morning," Ashe says, rocking the baby's carrier, trying to keep her asleep.

"Look" I begin gently. "I appreciate this. I really do. You're all incredibly thoughtful and welcoming, but…I'm just getting out of what I can only describe as hell on earth."

"I swear," Keira grinds out, "if Locke wasn't dead already I'd string him up and go real slow and deep with my claws—"

"Keira," Julia says tightly.

I give the female an appreciative smile. I really like her. "My point," I say, "is that I'm not ready for fun and light and relaxing. I'm still trying to breathe right. I'm trying to figure out just who the hell I am."

For a moment or two the only sound I hear is the bayou rushing by, the baby smacking her sweet little lips together in her sleep, and my heart beating inside my chest.

"Three's name is Olivier," Genny tells me.

I look up, over at her.

"His mate, Shasta, died several years ago," she continues.

My throat goes tight. "How?"

"She left the Wildlands and went searching for him. Got mixed up with some bad people."

"Does he know?"

She nods.

I put my plate down and come to my feet. "I have to see him."

"No."

The voice isn't Genny's. Or Keira's. Or Ashe's. Or Julia's. It's all male. And it's deeply possessive and strikingly pissed off.

CHAPTER 7

Striker

"And I can't believe you're even contemplating this," I say as Twelve and I stalk each other in the living room of the cottage.

Gone are the females. Their picnic and their *news*. I'm fucking furious. At how Raphael could've allowed this information about one of the males inside the lab to get to Twelve when she's been out less than a week. And how he was zero help when it came to dealing with his mate. He couldn't have cared less that she was here talking to Twelve. All the male wanted to know was how his baby, Soyala, was doing. Was she asleep? Had she smiled for him?

My lip curls. The downfall of the Pantera male: a baby.

"He was as close to a friend as I had in there, Striker," Twelve is saying, stopping with her back to the window and glaring at me.

"I don't care," I say simply. Maybe too simply.

She shakes her head, her eyes fierce with well-earned liberty. "You can't stop me."

I sniff. "Watch me."

"I'll go to Raphael," she tosses out. Then rewinds and snorts. "Oh, fuck that, I'll go see Three, and you can go to hell."

This female is at her most beautiful when she's fierce, but I can't give in to her. "You are a walking pheromone, Twelve. Don't you get that? You're not safe out there."

"Fine. Then come with me."

I stop. Stare at her.

One dark eyebrow raises over those pale, icy blue eyes. "Your job is to protect me, right?" she says, and the thread of sarcasm is blatantly obvious. "So. Protect me."

My chin jacks up. "And if your 'friend' tries to fuck you?"

Heat slams into her cheeks. I wait for her to tell me to go straight to hell. I'd deserve it. Not that I'm taking it back—but I'd still deserve it. She walks up to me and forces a grin. "I might let him. And this time, with my mind intact."

With those words, I feel like I've been shot in the chest. A round of twelve bullets straight into my heart muscle. I shouldn't care. I don't want to. She can be with whoever she wants. I've taken myself out of the mix.

But I remember this morning. And last night, the last four nights…

I remember how warm she is, inside and out. How she knows pain, yet is willing to put it aside and embrace life and happiness.

The idea of another male…not just touching her skin, but being on the receiving end of all that goodness and grace…

Her stern gaze clings to mine, trying to read me. I don't think she can. I pray my conflict isn't written all over my face. Up until I met her, I was incredibly gifted at masking my emotions. Not so much anymore…

"All right," I say. "I'll go. I'll protect you."

It's like a vacuum came and sucked out all the fierceness in her eyes and her expression. Her shoulders fall and she nods. I hate it. I only want to see happiness and hunger and pleasure in those baby blues.

I head over to the door, pull the screen back. My gaze finds hers. "You wanna take the pumas?"

This gets me a small smile and a shrug/nod, but truly it's like the motherfucking sun has come out after days of rain. She has broken through my wall. Shrouded my past with the need to help her overcome her own. And as she walks by me, shifting into her puma as she goes, I feel weakened. Both in body and in mind.

I am the Hunter, yet she possesses all of the strength.

***

Twelve

I'm nervous. But not for the reasons one might think. When you see someone again who's been through the same war as you, someone who's experienced horrific things, shared incredibly personal things, it's like looking at an old home movie. The ones that show the hurt on people's faces through forced smiles.

I'm worried as I stand inside the clinic at the door to Three's room—*Olivier's* room. That I'm going to feel like I'm back there again. In the lab. The second I see him. And I'm not sure I can handle it. Or…I don't want to have to handle it.

"You don't have to do this now," Striker says. "Let's go back to the cottage. You can do this another day."

He's standing to my left. Despite our tiff earlier, he's been nothing but supportive, even though I know he doesn't want to be here either. For very different reasons, of course. Reasons I refuse to think about right now. Or hope will ever be resolved.

I shake my head. "I want to see him." Then I push open the door. The one thing Striker demanded was that he could stay inside the room with me. I was going to fight him on it, but I'm tired of fighting. And I did acknowledge him as my protector.

The room the Pantera have Olivier in is very similar to the one they put me in when I first got here. Sterile but warm, with a sitting area, bed, lots of windows. I spot him at once. That shoulder-length dark blond hair is a dead giveaway. He's standing over by one of the windows, staring out at the lawn.

"You remember it?" I say. "This place?"

He glances back and smiles so bright and so wide, I feel tears in my throat. "Twelve."

"Three." I rush over to him and throw my arms around his neck. He feels so familiar. Safe in a strange, delusional way. "Olivier."

"Ha!" He pulls back and looks down at me. He's got the warmest brown eyes, the gentlest smile. "It's a name I had to bury in the labs. Feels so strange to hear that name again."

I smile back. "I like it. It's just right on you."

A low growl echoes through the room. Olivier's eyes flicker past my shoulder. "Don't worry, Hunter," he says to Striker, who I can only imagine is looking all kinds of fierce right now. "We're old friends."

"Never mind Striker," I tell him. "He's harmless." Or he better be.

"I don't know," Olivier says. "With the daggers his cat is throwing me right now, and those fangs…"

"What?" I release him completely and turn around. My gut tightens.

What is Striker playing at? Gone is the male Pantera guarding the door. Now it's a massive black puma, standing sentry.

I turn back to Olivier and shake my head. "Come on." I take his hand and lead him over to the small table and chairs. "I can't believe you're here," I tell him, taking a seat.

He sighs, sits down across from me. "This is my home. Or was."

"I heard about your mate. I'm so sorry."

"Thank you."

"How long are you going to be in here?"

"Not long." His lips thin. "They just want to check me out, make sure I'm okay physically and…well, the mental soundness part might take a little longer…"

"Oh, I know."

He smiles sadly. "I'm sure you do. But that part can be outpatient. Ongoing." He studies me for a second. "It's faded."

My brows draw together. "What?"

"Whatever it was they injected you with. You know, to keep us…insane…crazy with lust…" He inhales deeply. "It's not completely gone, but it's manageable."

"Really?" My heart lurches into my throat. "Is that even possible? I mean, I was hoping, but…"

The relief that flows through me is massive. Goddess, what this means… I can walk around without worrying. No protection needed. I venture a glance at the black cat near the door. Its emerald eyes are rabid as it looks from me to Olivier. It doesn't like this news. *Well, too bad. You don't get to pick and choose how you get me. Lover. Protector. "Scandal" watcher. Friend.*

"You look good, Twelve," Olivier says, his gaze running over my face. "By the way, are you going to keep the name?"

"Depends. I need to remember the one I was born with first."

His eyes cloud over. "You still don't remember? Why…?"

I shake my head. "I don't know. It was coming to me, some things, a few things, but I believe to bring it all back I need—"

My words are cut off by a feral, deadly growl. I whirl around and glare at Striker. *Not your business, kitty cat. Back off.*

His cat narrows its eyes.

I turn back to Olivier. "Whatever those bastards did to me to turn me into a mindless breeding machine ninety percent of the time has had long-term effects."

"But you said the memories could come back."

"Yes. I believe so."

He leans in, takes my hand. "You saved me so many times in there, Twelve. What can I do? Anything." His eyes are pinned to mine. "And I mean anything. It would be my pleasure."

All I see is a black blur, feel Olivier's hand ripped from mine, then hear him drop on the ground. When my vision clears, he's on his back and Striker's cat is snarling above him.

"Stop!" I cry. "What the hell are you doing?" I'm on my feet, pointing at the door. "Get out! Right now, Striker. Leave!"

But the cat doesn't even look my way. Its eyes are fixed on Olivier.

"Shit," Olivier utters. "I haven't been able to access my cat yet."

I'm so angry. Poor Olivier has been through hell. This is the last thing he needs. I stalk over to Striker and get right in front of his puma. "Leave," I say through gritted teeth. "Stop being a selfish prick, and leave." Emotion is rising up inside me, making my head swim, but I push it away. "I don't need your protection anymore. Ever again."

The puma snarls, then shudders, then quickly shifts back into the male. He looms above me, his eyes narrowed on mine.

"How could you?" I start.

"He won't touch you," Striker grinds out. "No one will."

Fury replaces anger and I open my mouth to give him another piece of my mind. But a sudden blast of light hits my eyes and I'm struck dumb. On a gasp, I grip my head.

"What's wrong, Twelve?" Olivier is at my side in an instant, his hands on my shoulders. "What's going on?"

"Move away from her," Striker growls.

"Stop it," I utter through the pain. "You don't get to do this. Dictate who touches me and who doesn't." I squint up at him. My head feels like it's going to explode. "You don't want to help me? Then get out of the way for someone who does."

It's not like the crash of an ocean wave, the way my brain turns from lucid to survivor mode. It's more like a light switch. On one second, off the next. No time to be afraid. No time to prepare.

I'm just…gone.

CHAPTER 8

Twelve

I am the creature now. Stalking my prey. I want to play with my food. Lick and suck. But it won't let me. It tries to talk to me. Softly. Soft things I don't understand.

It puts its lips on mine.

That I understand.

And the hardness sliding inside me. That I understand, too. That is what matters.

All that matters.

I growl at it. Move and bite. I want more. I want to scream. I want to feel…everything…what I am—who…

Its lips want to consume mine, but I only want the hardness. What's inside the hardness. Why does it slow? It keeps making sounds—

"Look at me, Twelve," it says. Is it sad? Is it hurt? "Look in my eyes. You know who I am."

I don't understand any of it. Who is Twelve?

I wrap myself around it again and squeeze it. It groans, but won't release. Only hardness. No eyes. No sounds.

I am wild. I am...what? Feline? Is that something? Is that anything.

It is shaking. The hardness...I want...

"Fuck," it snarls above me. "I'm coming. Again. Come with me this time, Twelve. Come back to me."

What is this 'Twelve'?

Back...

I'm here. I'm...

And then thoughts are no more. I am being bathed in heat and wetness and light. I am stillness. It makes me feel...

Oh, I feel...

When it presses against me, I lean into its soft over hard and bite until it moves again. Hardness again. Until it gives me more.

More.

Always more.

***

Striker

I sit on the chair across from the bed, buck-ass naked, my dick tired. I've been fucking Twelve for eight hours straight, and she's finally asleep.

I can't believe myself. How I acted. How I've been acting for the past seven years. Selfish. Living under the ever-sagging roof of self-protection only to hurt the one female on earth I want more than anything to protect.

I drove Twelve back into madness.

The thought peels another layer from my gut. In punishing myself and Farrah and my brother, I ended up punishing this female I'm falling hard and fast for.

I want her. All of her. The realization hit the second she hit the ground. Which was too fucking late. I don't deserve her anymore. But I'm at least going to help her, give her what she needs, what she's wanted from the moment she could ask me for it.

What I was too selfish and afraid and pigheaded to give her.

She stirs then, and I sit up. I refuse rest. I won't sleep or eat until she's awake—until her mind is awake. Even if it means I end up mad.

Madness with her could be beautiful. I'd be happy in her world. I already am…was…

A soft growl erupts from the bed and I'm on my feet and stalking over to her. She senses my presence and instantly opens her legs for me. As tired as I am, my cock starts to fill with blood. It's addicted to her. Like the puma is.

Like I am.

I'm over her, pushing my shoulders against the backs of her thighs to give me better access. This will be the only thing I consume until she wakes.

The perfect feast.

She snarls and fists my hair, then shoves my face down into her sweet, ever-creaming pussy.

CHAPTER 9

Twelve

Twelve.

No.

Seleste.

Seleste Brihoni.

The light switch has been flipped. And this is no overhead fluorescent that's been turned on. This is a chandelier at an opera house. Grand. Exquisite. It's all there. Everything. Right inside my mind, totally available. Card catalog, baby. My name. My family's name. I have a sister. A dog named Guapo. He loves to run around and taunt the alligators. I am a Healer. Oh, Goddess, that's why I met with the doctor in Miami, the one who brought me to the labs, sold me. He had medicine I needed. Medicine I was hoping to bring back—

The memory sends a wash of adrenaline running through me. My eyes open, and I stare. At the ceiling? Moonlight makes shadows on it. Or is that the pale light from a lamp? I'm in the cottage. It's night. What happened? I'm sore. "How long…"

"Two days."

The male voice is familiar, and sends shards of white-hot electricity into my heart. "Striker?" I sit up, too fast, and instantly feel dizzy.

"Wait, wait…shit, Twelve." He's beside me in an instant. "Easy."

I look up at him in the pale amber light of a nearby lamp. "I've been out two days?"

He nods, his eyes thick with concern. He's got a shadow of a beard. He looks exhausted. He's naked. I'm naked.

I shake my head ever so gently. "Have I been asleep? In some type of coma…?"

His jaw goes tight. "No."

I force all those amazing memories aside for just a second. Just to access what the recent past has wrought. The creature, Striker…he's naked. I'm naked.

I glance down. I'm sore, yet satiated. My memories are there, so…

My eyes come back to his. "Oh," is all I can say.

"Are you thirsty?" he asks. "Hungry? I can get us something."

"No." I'm not. I don't know what I am exactly. "Thank you." I'm so formal all of a sudden. I feel vulnerable. And something blankets me. A coldness, a protective shell.

He sees it, understands it, and his face goes pale.

I move away, just a few inches, but it's enough. "Thank you for your services," I tell him, easing the blanket to my chest. "For taking pity on me and granting my request."

"Twelve—"

I shake my head. "No. My name is Seleste Brihoni."

His breath catches. "You know…"

"Everything. Where I'm from. Who I am."

"Seleste. Goddess, that's beautiful."

I hate the sound of it on his tongue because it makes my insides hum. Not just with desire anymore, or with hope, but with a deep sadness. We're over. No…we never even started. What happened with Three showed—

I find his gaze again. "Olivier?" I ask, a slight panic in my voice.

Shame coats those fearsome green eyes. "He's fine. Living in the Nurturer dorms. Wanting to see you whenever you're ready."

"He's a Nurturer," I say softly, mostly to myself. Like me. No wonder we found common ground and a friendship. My eyes cut back to Striker. "What you did to him—"

"I know."

"It was inexcusable."

"Yes," he agrees.

I release a breath. I'm suddenly weary. Emotionally drained. "Look, Striker. This week was difficult on both of us. We had things to face and deal with. But your job's over. I'm good. Healed." *Brokenhearted.* "We're done."

His eyes darken and I see the cat behind them. "I don't want it to be done."

My heart jumps to respond in kind—or maybe that's my cat. The feline is going to have a hard time walking away from this Hunter. I'm not looking back ever again. I have a future to see to. And he made it very clear that he's not going to be a part of it. "I got what I needed."

His nostrils flare. "Your memories?"

"That's not a small thing," I assure him. "You gave them to me, and I'll always be grateful."

"You're welcome," he says tightly.

"I hope you find happiness someday, Striker." The words are foolish and they bring emotion to the surface—emotion I've pushed down to get through this quasi-breakup. And yet, I say more. Can't help myself because this may be the last time I see this male. "If you can let go of the anger and fear that cages your heart." I nod, bite my lip to keep the tears quelled. "You will. I know it."

Before he can reply or touch me or show his cat, I'm scrambling off the bed. I need to get away from him before the tears come. No one gets my tears now but me.

"I'm going to take a shower. When I come out, I think you should be gone."

"Twelve—"

I don't look back. "That's not who I am anymore," I call over my shoulder. "Good luck, Striker."

***

Striker

Dawn came early for me today. I patrolled borders with Bayon and Mal, and had a meeting with Raphael regarding my trip to the Everglades. I'd pushed the leader to delay the trip a couple of days so I could stay with Twelve—with Seleste. Goddess, that name suits her. I told him he could send someone else if he wanted to, that my place was with her. But he gave me the time, despite the danger we face, and the new concern over not only what Xavier discovered on Locke's damaged disk drive but his belief that there might have been a copy made. It looks as though healing sick rich people with our potent blood was just the tip of the iceberg. Military involvement, super soldiers…all of that shit is coming. I need to get to the Everglades. The bayou Pantera need to gain allies for the fight ahead.

I've been booked on an eight o'clock flight tonight. Along with Pride and Shadow. But first I have a wrong to right.

"Your cat is pretty damn powerful, Hunter," Olivier says when I drop down beside him near one of the massive cypress outside the Nurturer dorms.

"My cat and I are idiots," I say. I turn to look at him. "I'm sorry."

He nods. "It's okay."

"It's not, but I appreciate the quick forgiveness." I release a breath. "I haven't acted like that since… Shit, I don't think I've ever acted like that."

The male laughs. "We do things like that, act like that, when we're in love."

"Love?" I say on a laugh. "No."

Pale brows go up. "You're serious? You're going to deny that? You practically took my head off for caring about my friend."

The cat inside me rakes its claws over some vital organs. "She isn't just your friend."

"That's exactly what she is. We helped each other survive." He turns to face me, fully. "What happened to us, Striker, what we did, that wasn't fucking. And it sure as hell wasn't making love. It was torture, devised by a brutal, ruthless piece of shit who I'm beyond thankful is dead." His breath catches in his throat, but he presses on. "Twelve and I, we lived through that. Neither one of us wants to go back. Hell, none of the rats here want to relive that time. The future is all we see now. All we want to see."

I'm thrown. Sickened. By myself and what this male has just said to me. To live through that and come out again. Not jaded, but hopeful.

I get it.

Fuck me. I so get it.

"I want to see that too," I tell him. "The future." My lips twitch. "With her."

He smiles broadly at me. "Good."

"Thanks, brother. For what you did." I reach for a quick clasp of his hand.

He gives it to me, but looks confused. "What was that?"

"Helping her. Being her friend." My chest is tight. Emotion will do that to you, I guess. It's been a long time. "Getting her through so she could know freedom again. And," my damn voice breaks, "so I could know her."

Olivier nods kindly. "Just remember, no one wants to go back. Be reminded of all that was lost. At least until they can put it away for good and move on."

"Maybe I can help with one thing that's lost," I say.

"What's that?"

I push away from the tree and stand up. "Your puma. You remember him?"

The male's eyes get watery in an instant, and he turns away. "Oh, I sure do. The king of the bayou. Massive shoulders, auburn coat. Black eyes." He looks up at me. "But I don't—I can't access him."

"That's what Seleste said too."

"Who's Sel—" He pauses, then understanding dawns and he smiles. Wide. "Is that her name?"

"Gorgeous, isn't it?"

He nods. "Fits. I'm glad she got her memories back."

"Me too. Just hoping I don't become one of them."

Olivier laughs.

I grin. I think us two could become friends. "All right now," I say. "We're going to find that cat."

And with a shudder, I shift into my puma and roar.

CHAPTER 10

Seleste

I don't have much—a few clothes, the iPad. But then again, I have everything. My memories. My mind. I know the latter might continue to fade out on me… Who truly knows the long-term effects of the experiments I was subjected to and the drugs I was given? But I'll take it one day at a time, deal with each obstacle as it comes my way.

With my family by my side.

I zip up the bag Dr. Julia gave me and smile. Speaking to them this morning was the greatest gift I've ever been given. My mom cried for three solid minutes, while my father kept saying my name, over and over again.

Tears prick my eyes and I swipe them away. *Tonight. You'll see them tonight.*

I head into the living room just as there's a knock on the cottage door. It sends both thrills and sadness to my insides. Raphael has enlisted Keira to travel with me to the Wetlands. I told him it wasn't necessary, but he insisted. To be honest, I wouldn't mind the company. It's going to be very difficult for me to walk away from the bayou. From him…

Him. Striker. The male who has both stolen my heart and refused it. The male who gave me my history back.

The male who is right now standing at my front door.

I stare at him, open mouthed, my heart kicking in my chest. First, because I'm surprised. And second, because he looks absolutely gorgeous in black jeans that encase his long, powerful legs, and a gray fitted T-shirt. I put my fingers to my mouth to check to see if I'm drooling.

Then quickly remove them when I remember what's gone down between us.

"Why are you here, Striker?" I ask.

His eyes are completely pinned to mine. They're different somehow. Not softer exactly, but maybe…vulnerable? Is that even possible?

"I'm going to take you to the airport."

"What?" Goddess. So, he's already heard I'm going home. Is he sad? Hurt? *Dammit, female! Why do you care? He. Doesn't. Want. A. Relationship.*

"Bags packed? Or," he glances past me. "Bag?"

I shake my head. "No."

"Well, you better get on that."

"No. I'm saying that Keira's going with me."

He doesn't seem even remotely surprised by this news. "Why should Keira go when I'm already taking that flight?" He leans against the doorframe, one dark brow raised.

My heart drops into my gut. "No."

"Yes."

"Why?" I hate that my breath has left my body. I hate what my mind is conjuring…

"The trip was already planned a week ago," he says. "A meet and greet with your Cadejo."

Foolish disappointment slithers through me. A planned trip. So, it's more convenient for Striker to take me. Don't need to use up another Hunter's time or energy. I'm such an idiot. "I'm sure they'll be interested to talk with you. How many days will you be there?"

"Depends." His eyes fairly burn into mine.

I shiver. "On?"

"You."

My heart seizes inside my chest, but I force a laugh. "What do I have to do with any of this? I'm just going home."

He cocks his head. "I'm hoping it can be my home too." Once again, that…vulnerability that I saw in his gaze earlier is back.

"You want to leave the Wildlands?" I ask softly.

"I want to be wherever you are, Seleste. I love you. So much it hurts. No." He shakes his head and grins. "That's not right at all. It doesn't hurt. It's the opposite of hurt. It feels amazing. So fucking good I refuse to be without it ever again." His eyes find mine again and hold. "I refuse to be without you."

I can't believe what I'm hearing. What he's saying. My breath is caught in my lungs, and tears are burning in my eyes. This is so cruel. "Don't," I tell him, turning away. I leave him standing there and walk back inside the cottage.

He follows me, leaves the door open. "I have to. It's about time I said it."

"No, it's not! It's too late."

He reaches for my arm and turns me to face him. "Never too late." His eyes delve into mine, silently begging me to listen. "Not to tell someone how you feel about them. How you think about them every second. How you thought your heart was dead, and then they came along with their beauty and their humor and their kindness and 'Scandal'—"

"Please, Striker." It's my turn to beg now, my voice breaking as tears stream down my face. "Please stop this."

"I can't stop, honey." He reaches for me, gently eases me into his arms. "I'm asking you to forgive me. I'm asking you to hear what's on my heart. How I've been a massive fool, so terrified of getting hurt again, that's exactly what happened. I hurt you and I hurt me."

I can't speak. I'm shaking my head, wishing he would stop, praying he won't.

"Will you let me spend a lifetime making up for it, Seleste?" he asks, his hands on my face now. He's looking at me with such softness, such…love? Can that really be true? "Let me prove I'm worthy of you. I'll do whatever it takes. However long it takes. Just let me be close to you."

There's fear that runs deep in me too. Of being hurt. Betrayed. But I've never allowed it to carve out my path. Striker did. And look where it got him. Begging for love.

I shake my head. Begging for a love that was his from day one.

That will always be his.

I turn my head in to his hand and kiss the palm. I hear him exhale. I hear him say my name. I feel his lips on my hair.

"Can I take you home, Seleste?" he whispers.

I nod through my tears.

"Can I meet your family?"

I nod again.

"And may I ask their permission to mate you?"

That brings my head up, and my eyes to his. Because that was it. The one thing that took Striker out of his past. Asking me to be his future.

"Yes, you may," I say through my tears. "My love. My Male. My mate."

Striker, the hard, gorgeous, kickass Hunter of the Pantera, has tears in his eyes, too. That's what happens when you let go, when you forgive, when you allow yourself to love.

"Should I get my bag?" I ask him, then break into an enormous grin. "I have the iPad. We can watch 'Scandal' on the plane."

"Best idea ever," he says, then reaches down for my tank top and pulls it over my head. He tosses it on the chair. "But first…"

I give him a look of mock shock. "The door's open."

He leans in and kisses me. "So?"

I smile. "Haven't you had enough of me, Hunter?"

"Not possible, Healer." With quick hands, he strips me bare, himself too, then spreads me down on the couch. "Legs around me, Mate. We only have thirty minutes and I intend to use every one of them."

My entire body flares with heat, and I instantly do as he commands.

"Goddess," he whispers, poised above me. "I've wanted this so badly."

"Making up?" I ask, staring into his eyes.

"No, my beautiful, Seleste. Making love."

As he slides inside me, filling me, so deep it steals my breath, his mouth covers mine in the sweetest, gentlest, most loving kiss I've ever known.

ABOUT THE AUTHORS

Alexandra Ivy is a New York Times and USA Today bestselling author of the Guardians of Eternity, as well as the Sentinels, Dragons of Eternity and ARES series. After majoring in theatre she decided she prefers to bring her characters to life on paper rather than stage. She lives in Missouri with her family. Visit her website at alexandraivy.com.

New York Times and USA Today Bestselling Author, **Laura Wright** is passionate about romantic fiction. Though she has spent most of her life immersed in acting, singing and competitive ballroom dancing, when she found the world of writing and books and endless cups of coffee she knew she was home. Laura is the author of the bestselling Mark of the Vampire series and the USA Today bestselling series, Bayou Heat, which she co-authors with Alexandra Ivy.

Laura lives in Los Angeles with her husband, two young children and three loveable dogs.

Made in the USA
San Bernardino, CA
16 June 2015